17 95

BIG SKY
DREAMS

BIG SKY DREAMS

•

LAURI OLSEN

AVALON BOOKS
THOMAS BOUREGY AND COMPANY, INC.
401 LAFAYETTE STREET
NEW YORK, NEW YORK 10003

PRINTED IN THE UNITED STATES OF AMERICA
ON ACID-FREE PAPER
BY HADDON CRAFTSMEN, SCRANTON, PENNSYLVANIA

For Melissa,
the source of my greatest pride,
who knows dreams do come true.

And for Gary,
whose smile is my sunshine
and whose love is my universe.

Chapter One

N o, it wasn't the Ziminski place anymore.

Frost-filled air amplified the grind of shifting gears as the parcel service van crunched along the snow-rutted lane and disappeared over the ridge. It wasn't quite six o'clock, yet the sun had already fled the pewter Montana sky, seeking sanctuary behind the white-blanketed Bridger Mountains.

Hinges screeched in frozen protest as Laura Carey pushed her way through the gate. Mincing her steps up the icy path to the house, she precariously steadied her parcel on one hip while maintaining her balance.

"So you're the little lady who bought the Ziminski place," the delivery man had observed. "Somebody mentioned you're from New York City."

"Manhattan." The limits of anonymity in a rural town were apparent.

It isn't the Ziminski place anymore, she reasoned defensively. *It's* my *place, and I'm working darned hard to pay for it.*

How long, she wondered, would it take the neighbors to identify the place as hers? How many calving seasons and branding parties and schoolhouse dances would pass before the area ranchers would give directions by pointing out the "Carey place"?

It had been hers almost four months now. The locals, however, still referred to the small acreage by the name of

1

the former owner whose Polish parents had homesteaded this small chunk of paradise at the turn of the century.

Illuminated by the welcoming porch light, the cozy white frame house exuded a warm glow in the western twilight. Frigid air guided the chimney smoke into a straight, purposeful column. By midnight, according to the weather report, the thermometer would dip to twenty below zero.

Inside, fire logs crackled invitingly, their reflection dancing across the oak floor. The room was toasty warm and held an underlying aroma of mint tea.

Laura shook the parcel gently after recognizing Kelly's return address. She ripped the wrapping paper in one smooth move and fed the flames with the wad. Licking tongues of fire devoured the fuel and spread puffs of heat across the woman's smooth olive skin as coppery highlights glinted in her thick brown hair.

As college roommates, Kelly Hancock and Laura had shared small tokens and holiday hugs. When Laura sat on a sandy Tunisian beach during her Peace Corps stint, Kelly had remembered her with warm hand-knit mittens and a Christmas card reading, *These are for when you bring your warm heart and cold hands back to New York.*

Now, Laura was delighted to discover more of Kelly's handiwork. She inspected the small bronze German shepherd sculpture closely, turning the mahogany base carefully.

In one fluid motion, she dived for the phone and punched in the number at Kelly's studio.

"Kelly, he's wonderful!" Laura cradled the phone against her shoulder while she admired her gift. "Your work gets more fantastic all the time."

"Honed to an expert degree?" Kelly quoted her latest review in a pseudo-haughty voice and then chuckled. "Well, pal, you've always said you wanted a dog. Now all your dreams are fulfilled—a place in Montana and a dog. This one won't cost much to feed!'' The redhead laughed with the irreverent, bubbling mirth Laura remembered best.

Minute gradations in the dog's fur, incredibly lifelike, caught the light. Kelly had captured the form and muscle tone of the dog perfectly.

"Gosh, I miss you, Kell. I still forget I can't just pick up the phone every time I want to tell you something or plan something to do after work." Laura visualized Kelly's clay-covered hand, inside a bread bag, holding the phone in her studio. Kelly never did anything without the omnipresent plastic bags keeping modeling medium from staining everything in her SoHo studio.

"Hey, I told you to vacation in Montana and live in Manhattan," Kelly reminded her. "But nooooo. You had to turn pioneer on us."

The gang at the television station had pleaded and cajoled too. But in the end, the day had arrived when Laura's video editing board and its accompanying maze of electronic components were loaded into the back of her car. What courage it took, in retrospect, to leave a blossoming career in television production to pursue her dream.

Leaving Alex wasn't that hard, Laura realized. Their year of dating had been lukewarm at best and lacking in something Laura couldn't pinpoint.

Saying good-bye to Kelly had been hard. Good friends, friends on whom one could depend and trust, were a precious commodity. Friends they would stay, Laura had promised the wet-eyed redhead.

"You're going to come visit me in Montana. Me and my dog," Laura corrected, "and we'll ski in the winter and pick huckleberries in the summer. We'll eat ourselves crazy and chase cowboys. You'll love it."

Despite the distance separating them both geographically and philosophically, Kelly hadn't forgotten. A place in the country and a big dumb dog, Laura had envisioned when they dreamed. She stroked the bronze sculpture lovingly. Long after her call to Kelly, Laura was still smiling over things they'd laughed about.

She put on a CD and sang along with a country-rock tune while she changed into a sweat suit. This was as close to Christmas as she was going to get. She had work to do. Mortgage payments didn't take a holiday, she told herself sagely.

The wind picked up outside, driving snow against the house siding and whispering under the crack of the front door. Rolling a throw rug, Laura poked it against the threshold and extinguished the draft.

This is the home I dreamed of. I did the right thing, Kelly, she reflected. *This is what I want.*

Then why, Laura asked herself, staring into the insolently snapping logs, *do I feel so alone?*

"Cold enough for you?"

Laura tapped fresh snow from her boots and stepped into the warmth of the small grocery store.

"Plenty cold," she answered, rubbing mittened hands together. "If this keeps up, Santa'll need to jump-start those reindeer tomorrow night!"

Agnes Stillman stocked the store shelves with canned goods while trading banter with her customer. "Oh, honey," she said laughingly, "nothing keeps Santa away. He'll be here, won't he, Jason?"

The gangling youngster balanced on the top rung of a wooden ladder as he threaded colored lights in the store-front window.

"There ain't a Santa Claus anyway," he scoffed, then showed the tin grin of corrective dental work in progress.

"Since when?" Laura feigned shock. "He always came when I lived in New York. Are you telling me he won't find me in Montana?"

"Maybe," the boy responded. "Everybody knows how to find the Ziminski place."

"Hey! It's the Carey place now," Laura reminded him. "And you can be sure he'll find me."

"Are you coming to the community program tonight, Laura?" Agnes emptied a case of soup and began shelving cans of corn. "Jason's going to do a reading. Our Homemakers' Club is raffling a quilt."

Laura glanced at her watch. "I really hadn't planned on it. I have some errands to run before the stores close, then I want to get home before dark."

"Better stay in town and come to the Christmas program, Laura," Jason called from his perch on the ladder. "I've been practicing my part for a month!"

"Why don't you come back after you've finished your errands, and have a bite of supper with us?" Agnes suggested. "Then we can all go to the program together." Nobody, Agnes reasoned, should be alone around the holidays. As a young bride, Agnes Stillman had spent Christmas by herself while Carl was stationed with the Marines in Vietnam. She knew the heartache of sitting home alone while families enjoyed holiday festivities. "We'd love to have you join us."

"Great!" Laura conceded. "You know I'm a rotten cook, but if I can help with dishes, I'll join you."

"Come back when you get your business done in town. We're closing the store early tonight. Carl's already shut off the gas pumps."

The family operation was set off the highway at the edge of town, and in addition to being a grocery mart and filling station, it served as the unofficial social center of town. When the pumps shut down at Stillman's, the streets of town were rolled up for the night.

"Let me get to the office supply shop and pick up what I need, and I'll be back in half an hour." Laura's spirits soared. She hurried through the snowy streets, smiling hellos at her fellow shoppers. Three or four people called her by name. The rest issued Christmas greetings with the same friendly cheer she had come to know in this part of the country. She smiled to herself. *Cold climate, warm hearts.*

"Laura, are you sure you won't have more biscuits?" Agnes offered when the roast beef, potatoes, and salad had disappeared. "You could use some meat on your bones."

Carl Stillman admonished his wife. "Now Agnes, don't push your biscuits on Laura. Look what they've done to me!" He patted his rotund stomach contentedly and flashed a look of sheer adoration at the cook.

"I'm stuffed. Agnes, nobody does pot roast like you do. No wonder Carl's such a happy soul." Laura flashed a grin at her friend across the table as he sopped up another serving of gravy and biscuits. "The way to a man's heart, you know!"

"How come you're not married?" Jason's voice interrupted Laura's reverie.

"Jason!"

"It's all right, Agnes. It's a legitimate question. After all, I'm a little long of tooth for a maiden lady."

"But it's none of your business, Jason," Carl reprimanded the boy.

"I never took the time, Jason." Laura grinned. "I was so darned busy with college, and then I went to Tunisia with the Peace Corps. By the time I got back to the States, I got started with filmmaking. I guess you'd say that's been my first love. Now I'm twenty-nine and very independent. I don't think anybody'd put up with me!"

"I bet you'll get married sometime and have kids," Jason speculated. "Maybe even learn to cook. Besides, twenty-nine isn't real old. Mom was forty-one when I was born."

"Jason!" Carl pushed his chair back and glowered at his son. "Help me bring in some firewood."

"Jason usually has better manners than that," Agnes apologized when the boy was out of hearing range.

"Think nothing of it. Children are naturally curious."

Agnes snorted and shook her head. "Nosy," she corrected. "Jason was being downright nosy."

"I didn't mind his asking." Laura scraped dishes and wiped the table clean while Agnes filled the sink with suds and tidied the kitchen.

"He's just fascinated with you." Jason's mother leaned conspiratorially towards Laura. "I heard him telling Danny Raoli the other day he thinks you're a fox."

"He's a great kid. Gosh, is he growing!" Laura added. "He's sure sprouted up in the four months I've known you."

"I remember before you came to the valley, the realtor told us you worked in a television studio in New York. Jason looks on you as quite a celebrity, you know."

"But I'm only a video editor. Nothing glamorous about that," Laura explained. "It's just a job, the same as you and Carl running the store."

"The only time Jason's been out of Montana is for the rodeo in Laramie," Agnes revealed. "You can imagine anybody from New York would seem pretty big time to him. And to me, too."

"You're the best," Laura reassured her.

"I know." Agnes grinned.

Red and green lights were twinkling their welcome to the Community Center when the Stillmans and their guest entered the hall. The scent of pine boughs decorating the stage mingled with the aroma of hot cider brewing in the kitchen. Holiday greetings volleyed from one group to another as the crowd filled folding chairs to watch the program.

"There's Shirley Nygaard, the town's librarian." Agnes pointed to a handsome woman of sixty-something. "She organizes this each year. She's also president of our history club. We meet on the second Thursday of each month if you're interested."

"Count me in. I'm anxious to learn all I can about the state," Laura said enthusiastically.

"Mom, can I sit with Randy and his family?" Jason's eyes were bright with the excitement found only in a twelve-year-old at Christmastime. Not waiting for an answer, Jason and his school friend poked their down-filled jackets under their arms and moved to a row of chairs nearer the stage.

"Carl! Agnes! Merry Christmas!"

A middle-aged couple enveloped the Stillmans in clumsy embraces, then turned to Laura.

"Jim Trask, and my wife Becky," the barrel-chested rancher introduced himself and the smiling lady at his side.

"Laura Carey."

"You're the one who bought the Ziminski place!" Becky chimed in. "We feel like crumbs that we didn't get over to meet you when you moved in. Seems like during harvest we don't get anywhere but the fields."

All married people grow to look like their spouses after a number of years, and the Trasks lent credibility to that theory. They stood before Laura with their matching broad smiles, weather-beaten faces, and sparkling eyes.

"Well, I don't get out much. I'm pretty tied to my editing board. Every time the UPS man comes, he brings me more work," Laura explained. "If it weren't for my occasional twinge of conscience that takes me to church, I wouldn't even have met Agnes and Carl!"

"Well, we're going to change all that," Becky assured her. "We're having an open house after the holidays, and we'll get you introduced to the rest of the folks around here!"

"Howdy!"

"Happy Holidays!"

"Good to see you!"

Greetings rang throughout the hall, until the lights dimmed and the program began. The lower grades were first to present their skits. A brief scuffle between two winged angels ended when one's mother bounded from the audience to retrieve her little cherub from the stage. A second-grade Mary and Joseph entered on their way to the stable, but when Joseph forgot his lines and began to cry, Mary was left to fend for herself. Then the fifth- and sixth-graders displayed their talents, with Jason's reading closing the school portion of the program.

"Help me put out cookies?" Carols had been sung after the show ended, and Agnes was in charge of refreshments. She and Laura joined the women in the kitchen while the men discussed crops and cattle prices. Children beyond control with the anticipation of Christmas filled the Community Center with a cacophony of shouts, giggles, and play.

Laura deposited a heaping tray of cookies on the buffet table and marveled again at the amount of food people had furnished for the community affair. There was no small amount of competition surrounding the donation of cookie trays; each contribution seemed to outshine the tray before it.

"Those look good enough to eat."

Glancing up, she met laughing blue eyes gazing longingly at the plate of cookies.

A real Montana cowboy, Laura mused. She took in his pearl-snapped western-cut shirt tucked into tight blue jeans and the leather vest spanning a broad chest. He stood eye level with Laura, who had always been slightly self-conscious about her five-feet, ten-inch height.

"Help yourself," she offered. "There's punch and coffee, too."

"Did you bake all these cookies yourself?"

"Good heavens, no! If I baked them, they wouldn't be fit to eat!" Video editing she could do. Baking, Laura figured, was a religious experience. If God had wanted her to bake, He wouldn't have invented Sara Lee.

"I'll bet your husband eats anything you bake."

Her glance skimmed down to his ringless left hand. "My, my, kind sir," she said, affecting a Scarlett O'Hara drawl and batting her eyelashes, "I've heard every little ol' pickup line outside of the Great State of Montana. Is this how you boys out West check to see if'n a gal's got a husband?"

Deep dimples pulled at his cheeks when he grinned. He cocked his finger at her, aiming it like a gun. "Bingo."

"Well, I don't have a husband," she answered. "And I've practically turned my oven into a planter. I'm certainly no domestic goddess!"

"Anybody with your looks definitely fits into the goddess category." He watched the red creep into her cheeks, and scored one for his own charm. He stuck out his large hand.

"I'm Butch Franklin."

"Laura Carey."

"Hey, you're the one who bought the Ziminski place."

"Yep. So now it's the Carey place. How about you? Do you live around here?"

He nodded and smiled, his cheeks creasing as his grin deepened. "My brother and I have the Flying G Ranch up the canyon. Part of our north pasture borders on the Ellis place near yours." He continued to hold her hand.

"Well"—Laura pulled her hand from his—"I hope to see you again, Mr. Franklin." He was cute. And they both knew it.

He ruffled his curly dark hair and looked directly into her eyes. "Butch."

"Butch," Laura repeated.

"Good evening, Barrett!" Ethel Bryant had taught both Franklin brothers in grade school, and she refused to use Butch's odious nickname. Moreover, no one had presented the newcomer in the valley to her. It was high time this young woman met Ethel Bryant.

"I'm Ethel Bryant. And you are . . . ?"

"Laura Carey. I'm pleased to meet you, Mrs. Bryant."

"Merry Christmas, Mrs. Bryant! Here, let me help you with that cookie tray." Before Laura's eyes, the macho, flirtatious cowboy had reverted to an eager-to-please six-year-old.

The old schoolteacher's eyes surveyed the room. "Where's your brother?"

"You know Morgan. He isn't much for parties. Takes too much time away from the ranch."

"It's high time he starts socializing," Mrs. Bryant stated emphatically. "He's becoming such a hermit I scarcely remember what he looks like."

"He's still tall and skinny and mean as can be!" Butch turned to Laura. "My brother was one of Mrs. Bryant's favorite students."

"One of the most brilliant minds I ever saw," the portly teacher reminisced. "You couldn't stump him in history. Morgan loves the subject. Well, Barrett, you tell him Mrs. Bryant sends him Christmas greetings. And now—" The blue-haired matron brushed her hands together and turned to leave. "—I'm needed in the kitchen."

"Merry Christmas, Butch!"

"Merry Christmas, Agnes!" He greeted Laura's friend with a hug. "Where's that rascal husband of yours?"

Agnes scanned the room. "Probably stepped out for a breath of fresh air. Have you met Laura?" Her arm went protectively around the young woman's shoulders.

"We just introduced ourselves," Laura answered, smiling at Butch. "And I met Ethel Bryant as well."

"I hope you stood tall, didn't chew gum, and didn't run

with scissors,'' Agnes joked. "Let's find a table and get comfortable." They filled napkins with baked goods and cradled them in their hands.

"Hey, go find yourself a wife and leave mine alone,'' Carl joked to Butch as he pulled out a chair and joined the group.

Butch recoiled in mock horror. "Don't hit me! It's just that Aggie's everything I ever wanted in a woman. She can cook, pull a calf, drive a tractor, and still smile like an angel.''

"Stop it.'' Agnes's punch connected with Butch's arm. "You're embarrassing me!''

"Now look here,'' Carl protested. "Here's a pretty gal right beside you and she's single!'' Both men laughed uproariously.

Butch folded his arms on the table and stared at Laura. "Well, how about it, Laura? Would you like to go out sometime?''

Take the plunge, Laura thought. *You've got to get involved in this community if you're ever going to fit in.*

"Sure, sometime . . .'' She kept it vague, in the event Butch had only extended the invitation at Carl's prompting. *Let him off the hook,* she told herself.

"How 'bout this snow?'' Butch shook his head. "It's really drifting up the canyon. We're supposed to have more tonight.''

"Six inches,'' Carl prompted.

"The windchill factor will dip well below zero tonight,'' Agnes added. "Oh, and everybody's invited for Christmas dinner,'' she offered around the table.

"Thanks, but I'm burning a turkey for me and Morgan.'' Butch grinned. "How about you, Laura? Would you like to join us?''

Laura shook her head. "It's another workday for me. I'm in the middle of a huge project that has to get done. But thanks.''

The coffeepots were refilled and conversation flowed throughout the noisy Community Center.

"What's Santa going to bring everybody?" Laura turned to Carl first.

"New leather mittens," he requested.

"An electric roaster big enough for a twenty-five-pound turkey," Agnes responded. "And a black nightgown!"

Butch held out one huge hand and started counting down on his fingers: a new pickup truck, a Hal Ketchum CD, a laser printer for his computer, and a bread machine.

"A bread machine?" his three tablemates reacted in unison.

"You think a man can't have kitchen gimmicks, too?" Butch asked, incredulous. "When it's Morgan's turn to cook, he won't make bread. The machine would be for him."

Carl turned to Laura. "And your wishes from Santa?"

Laura didn't have to think long. "A German shepherd puppy. Some good pearl earrings. And a nice sign to hang on the gatepost that says Carey, so everybody'll know it's not the Ziminski place anymore."

"You're easily pleased." Butch laughed.

"Oh!" Laura had another thought. "I also want a Burlington Award."

"What's that?"

"It's the industry's award for video editing. It's my ultimate goal to have one of those on my mantel someday."

"I know what you mean," Agnes supported her. "A woman needs her accomplishments recognized just the same as a man does."

"And your main accomplishment in life is being a good little wife," Carl joked, to the groans of both women.

"Oink, oink," they grunted between laughs.

The crystal-clear night was bitter cold when the party broke up. Agnes and Carl bundled into the front seat of their club cab pickup, with Jason and Laura huddling in the backseat while the defroster blew a clear semicircle across the windshield.

"What a great evening! Jason, you did a super job on the reading."

"Thanks. You did a good job serving the cookies," the youngster returned.

"And Butch Franklin did a good job of eating the cookies, once he saw Laura was serving them." Agnes laughed.

Laura pictured the rugged face with the dancing blue eyes that had clearly expressed an interest in her. "He seems like a nice guy."

"They *are* nice, both those Franklin boys," Carl agreed. "Butch has always been full of the devil. He was a terrible prankster when he was a kid. Never outgrew it completely. He loves a good time. Morgan takes life a little more seriously than Butch does, but that's not all bad. He's older, and he's always been all business."

Laura's car sat outside the store, dusted with a thin layer of snow from the huge flakes falling quietly in the valley.

"Let your car warm up a minute before you go," Carl reminded her.

Laura jumped in, cranked the engine, and let the defrosters go to work while she thanked the Stillmans again for the evening. "It was just wonderful," she said with a smile.

"Don't be a stranger!" Agnes called as Laura backed out of the driveway.

It felt good, getting to know the people in the community. Being here wasn't enough, Laura realized. It was the need of belonging, the sense of tribe. Inexplicably, she felt more at home here now, after four months, than she had felt anywhere in her life.

She steered through the snow on the highway while the wipers slapped away snow. *Silent night,* she reflected. *Holy night.*

Chapter Two

Laura awoke on Christmas Eve morning to frost-feathered windows and the distant sound of a snowplow on the turnoff road. Her sweat suit shielded her against the coolness of the house as she brushed her teeth and splashed some ambition onto her face with cold water. Breathing on the bedroom window, she rubbed a spot with her sleeve. As the pane cleared, diamond-like frosted clumps of field grass glistened in the golden light of morning. The serenity of the farmstead was the nicest Christmas gift she could've given herself, Laura realized.

In a spare bedroom turned into a work studio, stacks of broadcast tape awaited editing. The three editing assignments she had eagerly accepted for the extra income would supplement the mortgage payments she had incurred when she moved in. Slipping into place in front of her electronic board, she turned the machine on and set the digital counter for her input tape.

At noon, she stopped just long enough to brew a pot of mint tea and pull her hair into a makeshift ponytail. Then the work resumed: viewing footage, marking the beginning and ending edits, and transferring the results onto a second, or "dummy" tape. This particular project was a documentary on the train system in India. The videographer had worked with Laura before; he was well respected in his field and captured extraordinary images of antiquated locomotives and exotic train stations. Laura's hands flew across the board, deftly executing the cuts with practiced ease. It was an art, creating a finished film with each scene brought to perfect position before cutting to the next shot.

The late-afternoon sun slanted in the window, gradually sending more and more of the room into shadow. By six o'clock, daylight was gone, and the room had grown uncomfortably cool.

Laura switched off the editing board and straightened her back, cramped from too many hours at the table. She padded in stocking feet to the firebox next to the hearth, feeling chilled and relishing the thought of a roaring fire.

"Ho, ho, ho, Merry Christmas!"

She heard the deep voice outside at the same moment as she heard the front gate screech.

"Ho, ho, ho!"

From behind the curtain, she spotted Butch Franklin clomping toward the front door, his arms filled with green branches. She glanced at her reflection in the hall mirror. No makeup, messy hair, and a sweat suit that looked old enough to vote. *What a prize you are,* she told herself.

"Come in from the cold!" she greeted the smiling cowboy.

His nose was nearly as red as his plaid flap-eared cap, and his blue eyes watered when he hit the warm indoor air. The pungent smell of spruce filled the room as he set a small, full-limbed tree against the door and stamped snow off his boots.

"It's gonna get cold out there tonight!"

"By the looks of you, it already has!" Laura reached for his jacket as he shrugged out of it. He pulled the cap from his head and hung it on the doorknob.

"I thought you might need a tree. I drove past last night and didn't see any Christmas lights. I figured since you just moved here, maybe you didn't have any decorations."

"I've never had a Christmas tree before."

Had she announced her grandparents were space aliens, she could not have shocked him more.

"Never had a Christmas tree? Why wouldn't you have a tree?"

"My father had allergies, my mother didn't want the mess of dried needles"—she counted the excuses off her fingers—"and when I had my own apartment in New York, I just never found time to put one up."

"Maybe I should take this back to the ranch. . . ."

"Absolutely not," Laura insisted graciously. "It's a beautiful little tree, and I'm honored that you brought it."

"I just couldn't imagine you here alone on Christmas Eve without a tree. You are alone, aren't you?" Butch peeked around the corner into the kitchen.

"Alone and welcoming company," she answered. "Although I'm hardly dressed for company." She pulled at the faded sweatshirt.

"You look fine. You look like somebody who should decorate a Christmas tree!" Butch's enthusiasm was contagious. He placed the tree trunk in a container of sand he'd lugged from the truck.

"Want it in the bay window?"

"Sure." It was amazing how one small tree brought a holiday spirit into the house. They scooted it in front of the window seat and stood back to admire it.

"That's fine."

"It needs lights," Butch observed. It *was* a little bare.

"It's six-thirty on Christmas Eve," Laura reminded him needlessly. "Is any place open this time of night to get Christmas lights?"

Butch stared at her, his face rumpled like a crestfallen little boy's. "It didn't occur to me you wouldn't have lights." He brightened. "Hey! We've got some extra strings at the house. I used to decorate the trees in the front yard until they grew too tall."

"It's okay. I'd hate to have you make another trip up

the canyon tonight. Besides"—Laura glanced at her watch—"I was going to shower and go to Christmas Eve church services at eight."

"How about if I call Morgan and he can drop off the lights on his way into town? He mentioned going to services tonight too."

"Well, if you're sure he wouldn't mind."

"I'll trade you a cup of coffee for the tree, and then I'll call Morgan."

"Where are my manners? Of course, make yourself comfortable and I'll get you coffee." She turned in the doorway to the kitchen. "Or would you like something stronger? I make a mean hot mixed drink."

Butch smiled warmly. "Better make it coffee. If I go to church with Morgan, I'd better not be smelling of booze or I'll hear about it from him. He's not much of a drinker and he gets on me pretty hard if I party too much."

Laura switched on the coffeemaker and pulled a package from the freezer. Two minutes later the microwave beeped. *Ah, warm, delicious-smelling, nearly homemade cookies. Laura, your culinary skills abound,* she told herself. She piled them on a saucer.

Small talk mixed with the aroma of the cookies, the coffee, and the tree to fill the house with a holiday feeling. Butch's long legs, crossed at the ankle, jutted out into the middle of Laura's small parlor, emphasizing his masculinity. Resting comfortably in an overstuffed chair next to the fireplace, he was enjoying himself immensely.

"So you're taking a break from ranch work to bring a tree to the new girl in town. That's very thoughtful."

"Nothing like a pretty face to make a fella forget the cows!" His lighthearted response endeared him to Laura. "But," he added seriously, "we get things caught up around the place so we can relax and enjoy Christmas. Our family always had big Christmas celebrations. It's important to both Morgan and me to remember the holidays."

"What's your most memorable Christmas Eve?" Laura asked as she refilled his coffee cup.

"I was seven. Morgan was fourteen. I wanted a BB gun more than anything. Of course, our old man thought I was too young for one, so I got a play gun. Morgan got a .22 rifle. Boy, did it make me mad. So after everybody went to bed that night, I sneaked downstairs and took his rifle to the old outhouse by the barn, and dropped it down the hole. When they found out what I'd done, the old man spanked me, my mother took away my play gun, and Morgan fumed for a month. Years later, when I sold my first 4-H steer, I took the money and bought him another rifle. It's pretty funny now, but nobody saw the humor in it back then." He sipped his coffee and laughed softly. "How about yours?"

Laura thought for just a moment. "Probably when I was twelve. I had my eye on a doll I wanted more than anything, but my mom thought I was too old for dolls. Besides, she just didn't make a big deal out of Christmas. But when my dad came up to kiss me good night that Christmas Eve, he had the doll in a box for me. I can still remember how excited I was!" The glow in Laura's eyes rivaled that of the fireplace. "I named her Maggie. I still have her, and she has a place of honor on my bed.

"If you want to use the phone to call your brother, I thought I'd pop in the shower and do my hair before church services. Make yourself at home." Laura heard him phoning while she refilled the cookie plate and wiped off the counter. She could make out bits of the conversation.

". . . the old Ziminski place . . . never had a tree before . . . extra lights in the hall closet . . . stop by on your way . . . see ya in a few minutes."

"Morgan's bringing some lights for the tree," Butch hollered from the parlor.

"Great! I'm anxious to meet your brother," Laura called to him. "Is he as much fun as you are?"

"Heck, no!" Butch's response was instant. "He's terrific as a brother, but he takes life way too seriously. No wonder he's never gotten married. He'd bore a gal plumb to death."

"There are some CDs in the holder there, if you'd like some music while I'm getting ready." Laura nodded toward a stack of discs and left him to his own entertainment.

Hours of bending over the editing board had knotted Laura's back muscles, and she sought welcome relief in the enveloping luxury of a bubble bath. Her fingertips were getting pruny when she drained the bath and stood up to rinse off. The invigorating spray of the shower covered her voice as she sang Christmas carols and let the water massage her shoulders. She shampooed her hair, lingering under the warm cascading water.

Stepping out of the shower stall, she wrapped herself in a thick terry robe and rubbed her hair vigorously. When the long auburn mass was blown dry, she padded barefoot to her bedroom. Strains of a holiday compact disc sang from the parlor.

Did the people around here dress up for Christmas Eve services? Or did the weather dictate pants and sweaters even on holidays? Butch would know. Tucking the lapels of her bathrobe modestly up around her throat, she tightened her belt as she walked into the parlor.

"Butch, do I need to dress—"

"Not on my account, honey," was his response before she could finish.

At that same moment, she was startled to see they were not alone.

Standing just inside the front door was a tall, muscular giant with dark hair and a darker expression on his chiseled face. He looked like a cigarette ad come to life, in his black cowboy hat and sheepskin jacket.

"Laura, this is my brother, Morgan."

Glacial blue eyes froze a path from her face down the front of her robe, to her bare feet, and back to her face. "You don't waste any time, do you?" Morgan Franklin growled contemptuously. "You've known my brother for what, a week?" His look of disgust bore through her. "Sorry I interrupted you."

"I beg your pardon?" Laura gasped. Who in the world did he think he was talking to?

He dropped a bundle of Christmas lights on the chair and turned toward the door.

Laura was dumbstruck.

Butch was grinning from ear to ear. "Get your mind out of the gutter, Morgan. Laura took a shower and I've been sitting here listening to music."

The man rested his hands on lean hips and stared at his younger brother. "What am I supposed to think when somebody this good-lookin' "—he hooked a thumb towards Laura in derision—"parades around half-naked?"

"Morgan, I . . ." his brother began.

"Don't you dare explain, Butch!" she sputtered. "This is *my* house and if he doesn't like what's going on here— or what he *thinks* is going on—it's *his* problem!" Unaware of how wildly beautiful she appeared at that moment, with flushed cheeks and soft hair fanning across her shoulders, she crossed the room to confront Morgan. "How can you be so insulting? You don't even know me!"

"Morgan, you'd better apologize to Laura. She's a nice girl." Butch attempted to pacify her.

It didn't happen. She turned on Butch, her fury renewed.

"Hey, I am not a girl, I'm a woman. I'm not some brainless little toy you two can bandy around for your amusement." She confronted Butch with brown eyes that could've flashed lightning bolts. "You know darned well there's nothing going on here, so don't you *dare* give the impression anything improper is taking place. And you—"

She spun around and poked a finger at Morgan's chest. "—you . . . owe . . . me . . . an . . . apology." Each word was punctuated with her stabbing finger. "You wouldn't show another rancher the lack of respect you've just shown me." Color rose in her cheeks and her breath came in short, angry gasps. Who did he think he was, this giant of a man, jumping to conclusions and questioning her morals?

"Whoa!" Butch held up his hands in mock surrender. "Okay, woman," he emphasized the word, "I apologize for my brother's behavior as well as my own."

"Your brother is a grown man, Butch. Let him make his own apologies." Laura drew her bathrobe lapels nearly to her earlobes with great dignity and looked at her other visitor haughtily. "Well, I'm waiting . . ."

Morgan glared back at her.

A log popped in the fireplace.

A song on the CD instructed everyone to have themselves a merry little Christmas.

Butch looked from Laura to his brother, then back, as though following some convoluted tennis match.

The cowboy at the door exhaled with great flourish. "Sorry," he conceded.

"You should be," Laura snapped. "Now, if you'd care to sit down, I'll get you a cup of coffee. Then I'm going to finish dressing."

"Much obliged." He had removed his black cowboy hat again and stood with it in his hands, working the brim from one hand to another while the hat spiraled.

His discomfort was apparent. Was it the heated room, Laura wondered, or the embarrassing entrance he'd made, or was he just incredibly shy? Butch had told her his brother was thirty-four years old, and yet here he was, actually blushing. Well, let him blush. Let him melt in that heavy jacket!

After bringing his coffee, Laura excused herself, went

to her bedroom, and selected a long wool skirt, sweater, and high black boots. Her hands shook as she primped with her hair. The mascara wand darted around and finally imprinted a bar code–type smudge on her eyelid. *Goofy guy.* She shook her head. *He's nothing like Butch. Nothing at all.*

Returning to the parlor, she nodded toward the tree. "I'll decorate that tonight after church. And thanks, Butch. I do appreciate your thoughtfulness. And yours, too, Morgan." Her smile was a feeble attempt to smooth the man's ruffled feathers.

Both men stood as if on cue. The family resemblance was strong, although Morgan was a bigger, more weathered version of his younger brother. Years of outdoor exposure had etched lines around his piercing blue eyes and given his skin a leathery, masculine roughness. His jawline was firm. This man brooked no nonsense from anybody. He would be a formidable opponent, Laura knew instinctively.

Their mannerisms were different. Butch had a boldness forged from youthful exuberance and a touch of arrogance. His boyish charm, Laura guessed, had probably gotten him into and out of more scrapes than most men experienced in a lifetime. When all else failed, Butch would turn on the charm.

Morgan, on the other hand, appeared more guarded. There was something more, something indecipherable, in those cold blue eyes. Still waters, her grandmother had always quoted, ran deep.

"Ride to church with me?" Butch invited her.

Her glance encompassed both men. Morgan stood before her, still clutching his hat in one hand while the other massive fist incongruously held on to the delicately hooked cup handle. He watched Laura's every move; the wariness in his eyes didn't escape her.

"Morgan, perhaps you'd like to join us?" Laura offered.

"Thanks, no." He deposited the cup on the end table and fit his cowboy hat squarely on his head, shadowing the blue eyes that had scalpeled her earlier. He touched the front of the brim in greeting. "See you in church." A fleeting smile skimmed his lips before he turned to leave.

Not until she heard his truck drive away did Laura realize her hands were still shaking. Was she still angry at his accusations, or was it his size, his overpowering maleness, that had made her nervous? She only knew she was aware of the masculine strength of this man, in a way that struck a vulnerable chord within her. She hadn't sensed that feeling with his younger brother. Why did Morgan Franklin's presence fill the room so completely, and his leaving empty it so thoroughly? She didn't know, and not knowing unnerved her even more.

Chapter Three

Christmas Day passed much like any other day Laura spent at her editing board. She agonized over cuts, worrying about destroying a certain mood by leaving a scene at the wrong frame. So much of the documentary's impact depended on a smooth, unhesitating segue from one scene to the next.

She had confidence in her ability, yet the prestige of working on a Paul Caro production was a little intimidating. One of the country's foremost videographers, he set the industry standard in video production. Laura's work on a documentary in conjunction with the Boston Women's Health Cooperative had impressed him, and he was quick to call her upon his return from New Delhi. The fax lines were kept humming as the two discussed storyline, flow, and mood. The boxes of videotape Paul had sent lined one wall of her workroom. Bit by bit they were being logged in an organized, logical order.

New Year's Eve found Laura curled in front of the fireplace, reading a mystery and relaxing after another long day of work. In the icy stillness of midnight, she heard the faraway report of fireworks. How different this night was from last year's celebration! She and Alex had joined a party on the Upper East Side after stopping at a number of downtown dance clubs. Her sequined minidress that night had cost more than two mortgage payments on the farm.

Now the dress hung neglected in the closet while she ushered in the New Year in a gray sweat suit and wool socks.

The trill of the phone brought Laura bounding off the sofa.

"Laura?"

"Kelly!"

"I took a chance you'd be home. I thought I might get the answering machine if you were out on the town."

"I'm sitting in front of the fire all wrapped up in a good mystery." Laura remembered the two-hour time difference. "What about you? Did you go out and celebrate tonight?"

She heard a sigh. "I went out for a while with Raleigh. Remember him from Carson-Kellers?" Laura pictured the suave, ambitious executive from the accounting firm that handled the television station's books. She recalled salon-highlighted blond hair, buffed fingernails, and very expensive tailored suits. *Never trust a man with buffed nails,* she had wanted to warn Kelly.

"Remember him? Heck, it was at my birthday party you met him! I never would've put you together as a couple, though."

She heard Kelly laugh. "I know. You figured he was only interested in his mirror. But I saw him at a gallery showing last week, and since we were both without a date for tonight, we just decided to be lonely together. Who knows, we may end up seeing each other."

"Seeing each other?" He wasn't Kelly's type!

"Maybe." Kelly never hesitated an answer. "He's interesting and knows a lot about business."

Laura held her breath. Raleigh Newhall was a little too smooth, too . . . glossy. The fancy car, the imported shoes, the expensively capped teeth. Kelly evoked images of a romping puppy, energetic and delightfully disheveled. Laura couldn't imagine her friend falling for the ultra-sophistication Raleigh projected.

"You can't picture it, can you?" Kelly laughed. "The slovenly artist with the yuppie prince."

Laura sobered. "Nobody's ever going to be good enough for my buddy."

"Well, to be honest, it's just nice to have a date for New Year's Eve. What about you? Have you met Mr. Right?"

Visions of Butch Franklin flashed before Laura's eyes, then fled. Definitely not Mr. Right, not even Mr. Nearly.

"No," she answered honestly. "I went to church on Christmas Eve with a rancher I met at a community Christmas party."

"And?" Kelly waited.

"We laughed all the way home. He's great looking, two years younger than I am. A real joker with a terrific sense of humor. But romance? No. The chemistry's not there." As she heard herself recounting Butch's assets, Laura realized how much she enjoyed his friendship. At the same time, she couldn't imagine their relationship would ever move beyond the easy camaraderie they had established.

"Have you talked to Alex?"

"He's faxed me a couple of times. Newsy letters, nothing more. I guess he's accepted that I'm here to stay." The two women exchanged gossip and relived zany adventures they'd shared. An hour later, with promises to call more often, they said good-bye.

"Laura?" Kelly added as Laura was about to hang up.

"Yeah?"

"Happy New Year, buddy."

"You too, Kelly."

Long after the conversation ended, Laura stared at the twinkling lights of the spruce tree standing guardian in the bay window.

Rockefeller Center's lights would be blazing tonight. Times Square would be packed. The noise would be deafening.

The old farmhouse was silent, with only the crackle of the fire punctuating the stillness.

"You're a lucky woman, Laura Carey," she whispered to herself. Friends like Kelly and Agnes and Butch were worth their weight in gold. The film projects were going smoothly. She had plenty of firewood and a freezer full of packaged cookies. "Happy New Year."

Laura studied the mahogany-tinted face of the woman staring back at her from the videotape. A crimson sari stood out in stark contrast to the lush greenery of the Indian village. In accordance with that country's tradition, the woman had, upon becoming a widow, inherited her late husband's position with the government-owned railway. She proudly awaited the arrival of the train, when she would oversee the loading of the village's milk cans.

Scenes of the arriving locomotive were intercut with frames of the woman's face, drawing the viewer into the sense of expectation in the train yard.

The last tape of this segment had been pulled from the stack, and Laura felt deeply satisfied as she shut off the board. She glanced at her datebook, realizing that now, in the third week of January, she was nearly halfway through the project. It had been a series of twelve-hour days to get to this point, but she could visualize the finished program. It was one of the most exciting projects she'd ever encountered, and the time she'd spent on it was like child's play to her.

An invigorating shower revived her. Stepping into a forest-green velvet dress, she tied her hair into a cluster of curls with a matching ribbon. An invitation to Jim and Becky Trask's house party had come in last week's mail, and Laura had eagerly RSVP'd. At the history club meeting, Butch Franklin had suggested they attend together. *Why not?* Laura thought. He was fun to be with, and besides, he knew the route to the Trask Ranch.

"Anybody home?" Butch's voice called from the front step.

"Come in!" She hurried to the door, closing it quickly behind him to prevent the cold from entering the front room.

"Wow!" Butch's eyes traveled the length of her dress, then back to catch the shine of her hair and the sparkle in her brown eyes.

"Thanks!" One gleaming tendril danced across her cheek. Self-conscious, she blushed when Butch brushed it away. "Are you sure this is all right for the party?" she asked. "Not too plain or too fancy?" She pirouetted gracefully, sending the softly flared skirt out around her ankles.

"Perfect. Let's go. I've got my truck all warmed up."

"Looks like it's going to be another cold night." The mountains were silhouetted against the darkening sky. The snow moaned in crunching protest with each step.

"Probably ten below zero right now," Butch reckoned. Their breath hung in frosty balloons when they spoke.

Laura shivered. "I was hoping the cold would let up by now. It's almost the first of February."

Butch opened the passenger-side door and helped her into the pickup's cab, then circled around and climbed in beside her. A valiant attempt by the defroster kept the windshield frost-free.

"When the days begin to lengthen, the cold begins to strengthen," Butch quoted.

"Ah, just my luck—I'm partying with the Bard of the Mountains." Laura laughed. "Where did you hear that little ditty?"

"My Great-Grandma Gerard used to say it when January came. She and Grandpa homesteaded our place in the days when winters were really harsh."

Laura rubbed her gloved hands together. "I can't imagine any weather much harsher than this," she admitted.

Live music pouring from the ranch house greeted them

as Butch parked in the circular driveway and opened Laura's door. Party lights usually reserved for the Trasks' summer barbecues lined the walkway to the huge stone-and-cedar home.

"Don't stand out there in the cold," Jim Trask welcomed them from the doorway. "A guy could freeze on a night like this." He reached for Laura's hand and pulled her inside. As she shook off her coat, Jim motioned to the crowd-filled living room and stepped aside to let his guests enter.

"Hey, Butch!" A blond cowboy with thick glasses and a thicker mustache called to them.

"Hey, Ralph!" Butch responded with a grin. Introductions were exchanged, and someone handed Laura a glass of punch. Butch was rapidly drawn into an ongoing discussion with the group of ranchers.

"Can I dance with your girl, Butch?" another cowboy asked. Butch nodded, and Laura was whisked onto the dance floor by a stocky man whose two-step was amazingly light-footed.

"So you're the young lady on the Ziminski place."

"Yes." Laura introduced herself. "Now it's the Carey place," she added, smiling.

"Hi, Laura!" Becky Trask waved as she circled the dance floor with an older gentleman.

Laura nodded in acknowledgement, then braced herself as her dance partner whirled her around and pulled her back into his arms. The music ended and the party-goers applauded the five-piece band at the far end of the room.

Butch reappeared at her side with a plateful of food.

"Hungry?"

"Not really." Laura caught her breath. "I'm thirsty after that dance. I think I'll get a refill on the punch." She wound her way to the table laden with cold cuts, salads, and rolls. Both ends of the table held sparkling punch bowls.

"Watch that punch. It packs a wallop." Morgan Franklin issued a warning as he leaned closely over Laura's shoulder. His deep voice, characterized by that unique Montana drawl Laura had grown comfortable with, was smooth.

"Hello, Morgan." Laura felt a blush heating her face. She stood with the punch dipper midway to the bowl and turned to fill her cup. "May I get you some?"

He shook his head. "No, thanks. I'll stick to coffee."

"How have you been, Morgan?"

"Great. Butch tells me you're busy working on a documentary."

"Right," Laura confirmed. "It's about—"

"Morgan, we're missing a dance." Perfectly manicured scarlet nails clutched Morgan's arm, which then circled the pouting blonde's tiny waist. Her eyes glared icicles at Laura, then rolled coquettishly at Morgan.

"Laura, this is Janelle Harding. Janelle, Laura Carey."

"Pleased to meet you, Mrs. Carey," the blonde purred.

"It's Ms. Carey." Laura had never felt so tall and unfeminine in her life. The diminutive blonde stared at her as though Laura were the fifth face on Mount Rushmore.

"Laura bought the Ziminski place," Morgan explained.

"I just can't imagine a woman wanting to live alone in the country." Janelle made it sound like a felony.

Laura was uncharacteristically defensive. "I find it very peaceful," she responded. "It's paradise to me."

Morgan's steel-blue eyes scrutinized Laura while the blonde's arm snaked around his waist and her grip tightened.

Janelle's giggle sounded tinny. "The only way I'd be stuck out on some godforsaken spot in the mountains is if I had some handsome cowboy to keep me company!"

Oh brother, thought Laura. *Could you be a little more transparent, Blondie?*

"This cowboy would like company too," Butch announced to Laura as he circled her shoulder with his arm. "Come dance with me?"

The two Franklin men and their dance partners joined the throng. A waltz led into another two-step, then to a fast-paced jitterbug. Laura and Butch moved in perfect harmony, as though they'd danced together for years.

"Your brother's girlfriend is . . . um . . . interesting." Laura searched for the right adjective.

Butch snorted contemptuously. "Janelle's not his girlfriend. She's gone out with every guy in the valley. Janelle's got cowboy fever. Morgan just takes her out when he's tired of going places alone."

When the music shifted again, Laura saw Morgan striding toward them from across the floor. "Change partners?" he asked his brother.

Butch eyed Janelle Harding skeptically and nodded. "One dance."

Flushed from dancing and the excitement of the evening, as well as from the heat radiating from the huge stone fireplace, Laura's face glowed as she stepped in front of Morgan and took his hand.

At the first notes of the slow song, his arms enfolded her.

"I'm not a very good dancer." She gulped.

He held her tightly as they swayed to the rhythm.

"Be quiet," he ordered her. "You'll do just fine."

The clean smell of aftershave lotion lingered on his chiseled jawline.

His thick hair curled over his shirt collar and brushed against her hand. She could've raised her hand, Laura knew, and captured a handful of shining curls.

That he was the handsomest man she'd ever seen, she couldn't deny.

But the way she felt whenever she looked at him, was something she definitely wanted to deny.

This feeling was so unlike anything she'd ever felt before.

Unlike his brother, Morgan didn't speak when he danced. Laura silently prayed for conversation; maybe talking would take her mind off him.

Each moment seemed endless, yet she hoped the song would never end. The crowd, the room, all became a blur. The hypnotic, exquisite feeling of Morgan's arms around her led her through the dreamlike dance.

What's the matter with me? This is insane, she told herself. *I can't feel this way about somebody within the time span of one dance.* She missed a step, and Morgan leaned back from the waist and looked down into her eyes.

''Sorry,'' Laura apologized.

''My fault,'' he answered gallantly. His eyes held hers until she felt suffocated. Did he know what he was doing to her? Remarkably, Laura thought not.

It's the excitement of my first Montana holiday party, she rationalized. *That's all it is.*

Her peripheral vision caught Butch and Janelle dancing nearby. At the same time, the music ended. Morgan released her immediately.

''Thank you.'' His voice was husky.

Laura tried to speak. She was shaking inside and breathless. She clenched her hands and felt where his palms had been against hers. His touch lingered on her skin.

''I told Becky I was going to claim Laura for a dance!'' Jim Trask's voice broke the spell. Morgan turned to Janelle and led her off the dance floor, while Butch squired their hostess for the next song.

It was an evening of dancing and eating, visiting and laughing. Agnes and Carl joined them for a drink. Shirley Nygaard reminded her of the history club meeting the second week in February. They were expecting her to attend. Laura amazed herself at the ease with which she was fitting into the community.

"Hot coffee." Becky Trask served from a tray, fortifying her guests before they went out into the chilled air. After a round of coffee-cup chatter, the men put on their jackets and hats and went outside to warm up the vehicles.

"Becky, I can't thank you enough for your hospitality. This was a wonderful party." Laura shook her hostess's hand.

"We loved having you, Laura. You come see us anytime. And bring Butch along!"

On the ride home, Butch was animated. He sang along with the radio and retold jokes he'd heard at the party. And he reached for Laura's hand, holding it as he drove.

"Don't you need both hands to steer on these icy roads?" she joked. She was so comfortable with Butch. They could hold hands or not; it didn't matter. Talk came easy. He didn't make her nervous.

Unlike his brother.

When they reached Laura's, he kept the truck motor idling as he walked her up the path to the house.

"Laura, thanks for going to the party with me. I had a great time." He lightly brushed her lips with his.

It was her first kiss since she'd left Alex in New York, and it was a pleasant experience. Not spine-tingling. Certainly not earth-moving. But nice.

"Would you like to come in for a cup of coffee?" Laura offered.

"Thanks, but I'd better get home. The way the temperature's dropping tonight, I don't want to risk frozen water pipes. Better get home and plug in the heat tapes."

Morgan and Janelle had left the party ahead of them. The thought flashed through Laura's mind like an arrow, and hit its target.

"Maybe Morgan'll do it. He's probably beat you home," she suggested.

"Morgan had to take Janelle clear into town to her place. It'll be another hour before he gets home."

Long after his truck lights had disappeared over the ridge, Laura stood looking out the bay window.

Stars filled the black sky. Snow glistened where moonbeams played across the meadow. Despite the serenity of the farmstead, some unknown emotion knotted her stomach. It didn't make sense, and she certainly couldn't explain it. But she knew what was bothering her. Somewhere in town, Morgan Franklin was kissing some other woman good night.

Chapter Four

Laura scanned the poster on the door of the Community Center. Tonight's discussion: The reintroduction of wolves into the Yellowstone ecosystem. It was, Laura realized, a highly controversial subject, especially in the Gallatin Valley, where stock producers and pro-wolf factions were adamant in their views.

Her interest was twofold. The fascination she had for the powerful *canis lupus* dated back to the days when her father had kept her enthralled reading bedtime stories. The wolf, usually the villain, garnered Laura's sympathy. Intrigued by their beauty, their wildness, she anxiously awaited the scientist's lecture. She had seen wolves only in zoos around the world. Living in an area where they actually posed a threat fascinated her.

From both an artistic and a financial perspective, the potential for producing a documentary on the release program was great.

Arriving early to get a good seat, Laura went quickly to the front of the room. She took a spot in the front row and pulled a notebook from her oversized bag, ready to take notes. Within fifteen minutes, the center was filled with people.

"If I might have your attention . . ." The speaker adjusted the microphone on the lectern and the audience's collective murmuring and shuffling quieted down. "I'd like to get started on the program."

A brief history of wolves included Native American stories and European folklore. Some stories romanticized the beast; others decried his brutality.

Slides of wolves flashed on the screen, demonstrating the various postures the animals assumed depending upon whether they were playful, defensive, hungry, aggressive, or preparing to mate.

A multicolored map of Yellowstone Park outlined the release area as well as the expected pack routes. Laura noticed how near the park borders were in proximity to the canyon. The speaker told of elk herds that had starved the previous winter.

"When wolves were in the park, they kept the elk count at a manageable level," he reported. "Without the predatory wolves, elk populations have grown and their food supply has dwindled."

Additional slides showed bounty hunters from bygone days with their rack of wolf skins hanging behind them. Laura cringed as the image of the dead animals focused on the screen.

When the talk concluded, the discussion was opened to the audience.

"Can you predict how far the wolves will travel?" The question came from the back of the room. "Wolves won't stay where they're planted."

Murmurs of agreement filled the room.

"Any wolf that bothers my livestock's going to be a dead wolf!" The cattleman uttering the remark looked familiar to Laura. He'd been at the Trasks' party, where he had held court for anyone willing to listen to his views.

"Landowners on private property and individuals holding grazing permits on public lands will be asked to report harassing wolves within seven days. But keep in mind," the biologist pointed out, "wounded livestock or some remains of a carcass must be present with clear evidence that wolves were responsible for the damage. There must be reason to believe that additional losses would occur if the problem wolf or wolves were not controlled. You must realize such evidence is essential since wolves may simply feed on carrion they've found while not actually being responsible for the kill.''

The speaker folded his overhead projector into its case, signaling the end of his presentation. Remarks from the audience made it clear there was no consensus on the subject with this group.

''This is an issue on which, for livestock producers, there will never be peaceful coexistence,'' the biologist admitted. ''But the return of the wolves is definite. Ten pairs of breeding stock will be introduced into the park next month. They'll restore the natural balance of animals in the Yellowstone ecosystem. They're here to stay.''

In closing, he invited the audience to stop at the rear of the auditorium and pick up brochures from the information table.

Laura gathered a variety of booklets and was turning to leave when she glanced up. Morgan Franklin was in the crowd, his handsome head cocked to one side as he listened intently to one of the ranchers in his group. He nodded in agreement, his brow furrowed in concentration. As the group moved toward the door, Laura felt traitorous excitement as those mind-numbing blue eyes flashed in recognition when he spotted her.

The dark curly hair that had brushed her cheek when they danced a month ago had grown longer. His face was deeply tanned from the harsh winter sun's reflection off snow. In his thick sheepskin jacket, he looked as big as a mountain.

''Hello, Laura.'' His voice was soft but easily heard amid the voices in the hall.

Laura felt a flutter in the pit of her stomach but chose to ignore it. Why did this man affect her so? It was crazy. Why did she feel like a blathering fool around him? She couldn't even make decent conversation with him. Gone was the snappy repartee, the rapier wit she shot back at Butch when they were together. Around Morgan, she had no instant retorts. Her response to him wasn't the casual, glib give-and-take she had with Butch. No, Morgan Franklin tied her in knots.

He intimidated her.

He angered her.

And he fascinated her.

"How are you, Morgan?"

"Fine. Been busy with calving. You?"

"Great. I'm nearly through with a documentary I've spent a lot of time on."

"Butch mentioned you've been sticking pretty close to home with your editing. Didn't he tell me it's the Indian Railroad project?"

She was secretly very pleased that the two men had been discussing her. Did Morgan initiate it? Had he asked after her? She hoped so.

"Yes. He called last week and invited me to a movie, but I took a rain check."

"He's in Denver this week, buying bulls." His eyes liked what they saw as they covered her face.

"He mentioned he was going. I wish I'd had time to see him before he left, but I get so involved with my work I lose track of time."

The crowd moved around them as they blocked the doorway. It was apparent neither wanted to end the conversation.

"Look." Morgan glanced at his watch and smiled at her. "Would you like to come out to our place? I have to check cows around midnight, and I'd welcome the company if you want a cup of coffee."

No, Laura thought. *Let Janelle Harding keep you company. No, I don't trust the way I feel when I'm around you. No, I don't want to be alone with you.*

"Sure." Then reality struck. "Will my car make it up to your ranch?" Being one of the few inhabitants of the valley without a four-wheel-drive vehicle, Laura was cognizant of driving conditions when a storm front was in the area.

"I'll follow you to your place, and you can leave it there. I'll bring you back when you're ready." His hand on the small of her back guided her out the door into the freezing night.

The canyon was a moonlit fantasy. Towering evergreens stood tall and silent as sentinels uniformed with white snow epaulets.

A Beethoven tape sprinkled the truck cab with music.

"Good music," Laura commented.

Morgan turned to her with a droll smile. "It inspires me," he drawled.

"Beethoven and boots. Inspiration from classical music and dedication to a cow herd. Ethel Bryant told me you were the brightest pupil she ever had. You're quite an enigma, you know that?" Laura's tone was light, but she weighed every word before addressing him.

"How so?"

"You're so different from what I expected. You looked so angry the first time I met you. I got the impression right from the start you didn't approve of me. Yet from the little I've seen, you don't seem the judgmental type. I just don't know how to take you."

The driver's attention left the road for an instant as he leveled a glance at his passenger, then concentrated on driving as he answered. "It wasn't a question of liking you. You're beautiful and you're obviously very intelligent. But I've always been wary of strangers. It's one of the drawbacks of living in a small community your whole life. Butch tells me things are either black or white in my world. Maybe he's right."

"Butch is great. He's become a good friend."

"He wants to be more than friends," Morgan warned her.

"You're wrong," she countered. "I've made it very clear to Butch that I'm looking for a friend, not a man."

"That's part of your intrigue. You're the first woman he's dated that isn't just after his money."

"But we aren't really dating. We're just buddies."

Morgan's hands remained on the steering wheel as he shrugged nonchalantly. "Butch has got a lot of women chasing after him. But I noticed the night of Trasks' party he'd stake a claim on you if you'd let him. I just don't want to see anybody playing games with him." His voice was deathly serious.

"Let's get something straight." She turned to face him in the darkness of the pickup cab. "I'm a woman, not a possession. Nobody will ever 'stake a claim' on me. And don't think for a moment I'm playing some sort of game with him. I'm not after anybody's money. I can make my own. I don't play games and I don't believe in promiscuity!"

Morgan pulled his attention from the highway and grinned at her. "Good."

"Besides," she continued, "I believe in chemistry. I know when something's right for me. You know, my dad used to tease me because when he took me to buy my first bicycle, I walked in the store, strolled passed the rack of bikes, and picked out the one I wanted then and there," she recalled with pride. "I loved my little house the first time the realtor showed it to me."

"And the sparks didn't fly when you met Butch?"

"Butch is wonderful." *The sparks flew when I saw you,* she couldn't admit. Her answer was deliberately evasive. "I care for Butch a great deal."

That's it, Laura added to herself. *A great, caring friendship. Nothing more.*

The headlights caught the reflection of an animal's eyes, and Morgan braked to let three elk cross the road and scamper down the culvert. At the same time, his right arm instinctively flew out to prevent his passenger from being thrust into the dashboard.

"Thanks," Laura said softly, excited by the sight of the elk, yet relieved Morgan had protected her.

"You're welcome," came the reply.

The silence was deafening. Laura had to speak.

"Anyway, Butch was the first single guy I met after I moved here. I don't have the kind of social life that brings me in contact with lots of people. I'm pretty much stuck to my editing board. You must keep in mind that the only person I see for days at a time is Dean, the UPS man. I have to get out into the community. I can't be a complete hermit. That's another reason I've accepted dates with Butch."

"So you're available to other . . . suitors?" Humor underlined his choice of words.

"Sure. Introduce me to your single friends and I'll go out with them when I have time," she answered.

"But work takes priority?"

"Of course. Doesn't yours? Aren't you anxious to get home and check your herd?"

The sign reflected in the headlights pointed the turnoff to the Flying G Ranch.

"How do you know I'm not anxious to get you up there all alone on the mountain?" His voice was low, almost a growl.

He was laughing to himself, she knew, but the humor was lost on her. This wasn't Butch, Laura realized with something akin to panic. Morgan Franklin was a dangerous, unknown commodity. She had to bluff her way through, ignoring the way he made her feel.

"Because you only invited me so I can learn more about Montana ranching. Besides, I don't think Janelle would like it if she thought you were flirting with me.'' The moment the name came out, Laura dropped her joking manner. ''I do appreciate your showing me your ranch.''

She looked out the window and searched in vain for scenery in the dark as they thumped along the frozen, rutted road. Janelle Harding had come between them as certainly as if she were sitting in the middle of the truck seat.

They checked the pastures, lighted like day in the moonlight, and Morgan pointed to a number of cows which would, according to his predictions, calve within the next forty-eight hours. Walking fast to match Morgan's long stride, Laura relished her tour of the Flying G.

As he explained the duties involved in cattle ranching, Laura detected the pride in his voice. He was totally committed to this ranch, not only for his sake and Butch's. The heritage his grandparents had left them, it was his duty to guard. Despite falling cattle prices, increasing taxes, and threats from predatory wildlife, he would work this ranch. And someday, she knew, he would pass it to the next generation of Franklin ranchers: his sons or daughters.

Would they be Janelle's children too? Laura wondered.

Their conversation carried in the crisp night air. Laughter came easy in the moonlight. They competed to amuse each other. Laura delighted in his laughter, which bubbled from deep within him and softened the strong, serious planes of his face. He looked younger when amusement crinkled his cheeks and sparkled his eyes.

A handful of snow Laura scooped off the propane tank found itself carefully formed into a snowball and propelled to the back of Morgan's jacket. It landed with a thump.

''You're asking for trouble, Hotshot.'' His warning was tempered with a face-splitting grin.

''Nothing I can't handle, Cowboy,'' she answered, and swiped at the snow to form another missile. ''If I were you, I'd duck!''

The next moment, she was on the ground in the snow with Morgan's viselike grip pinning her arms beside her.

"Okay, city girl. Now what're you going to do?" He bent and rubbed her nose with his, Eskimo-kissing like children. He chuckled gleefully, like a carefree young boy. "Do you give up?"

Her hearty laughter echoed across the field. "I never give up!" She bolted suddenly, catching him off guard and wrapping her long legs around his. Flipping him on his back in the snow, she jumped up and ran toward the barn. "Never give up, never give up."

Her singsong voice sounded fainter as the distance between them grew. She became a speck in the moonlit pasture, but still he could hear her laughing and singing.

Morgan shook his head. She was the most fascinating woman he'd ever met. She was fun and sexy, smart and sweet. One minute she was the personification of big-city sophistication, then out popped an endearing innocence. Their conversation tonight pointed out, as had their previous encounters, her strength and focus. Had she ever needed anybody in her life? He didn't think so. She was completely independent.

Still, the rancher realized, it was a trait he admired in a woman. And this woman had spunk. She'd make somebody a wonderful partner in life. Maybe it would be Butch. She'd be a darned fine sister-in-law, Morgan reckoned.

He stopped in his tracks. Butch marrying Laura Carey? Why not? Butch was definitely interested.

Nope. It wouldn't work, Morgan argued with himself.
She's too independent; she'd walk all over Butch.
She's an artist.
Impulsive. Passionate.
Thank goodness she's Butch's concern and not mine, Morgan tried to convince himself.

* * *

The enormous gabled barn held several cow-calf pairs and as they entered, the smell of livestock and straw tickled Laura's nostrils. It was not unpleasant, she realized, and she found the earthiness of her surroundings stimulating.

"This is Rosebud," Morgan introduced her to a black Angus with a sturdy calf at its side.

The cow's dark eyes studied Laura as it chewed contentedly, then turned to care for its offspring.

Laura knelt before the calf and adoringly rubbed its velvety nose with her palm. Despite being raised in the heart of the city, she felt a magnetism for animals. She crooned softly to the critter.

The overhead lights of the barn caught the shimmering auburn of her hair as she stood in the stall, coming face-to-face with Morgan.

Unshed tears brimmed in her eyes. Her emotions had inexplicably plunged into overdrive the moment she had set foot in Morgan Franklin's truck. Rollicking in the snowy pasture with him, hearing him reveal his dreams, watching his eyes dance when he laughed, had only added to her confusion.

The realization raced through her mind: *what am I doing here? I'm alone with him. I'm vulnerable. I'm crazy,* she admonished herself. He was her only weakness.

He had invited her, she reasoned. And there was nowhere she'd rather be than here with him and his cow. "She's beautiful," Laura whispered.

Morgan's arms pulled her to him. "So are you." His voice was muffled in her hair.

Her arms reached around his neck as he lowered his lips to hers. Delight surged through her.

Morgan caught his breath, paused, and looked down at her. His eyes searched her face. They took in the heightened color of her cheeks. The combination of shyness and independence was a deadly combination in this woman.

''I promised you a cup of coffee. Let's go in the house.''
His voice held a smile.

The cold of the barn permeated Laura when she stepped out of the shelter of his arms. She had gone from exquisite warmth to freezing in a heartbeat, almost as though the kisses had never happened.

Chapter Five

The turn-of-the-century ranch house glowed with the charming patina of generations of loving family life. Furniture of exceptional quality, comfortably utilitarian but meticulously maintained, graced the room. A heavy oak dining table, extended from years of service to seat family and ranch hands, held a pottery vase filled with dried wheat and yarrow.

Sepia portraits hung in oval curved-glass frames suspended from ornate moldings near the high ceiling.

"This picture of my maternal great-grandparents was taken on their wedding day." Morgan pointed to the heirloom photograph. "Grandpa and Grandma Gerard. They started this ranch."

"The Flying G," Laura thought aloud. "Butch mentioned your Great-Grandmother Gerard. He frequently quotes her."

"She was quite a philosopher." Morgan chuckled softly. "She was tough, too. Had to be. Grandpa was gone a lot, buying and selling stock. She raised four sons almost alone."

"But a Franklin inherited the place?"

"My grandfather's brothers wanted no part of ranch life. They all went back East to make their fortunes. Grandpa Gerard married and had one daughter, my mother. The ranch was signed over to her when she turned twenty-five. It was her whole life."

"Is she still living?"

"She and my father were killed in a car accident a week after Butch graduated from high school. They were driving to Vermont to see an old family friend, and never made it. It was hard on Butch," he added unnecessarily.

"And on you . . ." She saw the hurt in his eyes as old wounds were reopened. It took all the strength she could muster to keep from touching him, holding him, helping banish the loneliness washing over his face.

"I was older. I had responsibilities. They'd have wanted me to keep going and take care of Butch."

"I think you still do."

He cocked his head to one side and looked at her. "I guess it sounds pretty crazy, but I still worry about Butch. I thought for a while I wouldn't have to. Did you know Butch was married once?"

Laura shook her head. "He never mentioned it."

"It's still a sore subject with him. It only lasted a year. He was twenty-two and thought he had all the answers. Maybe he did." Morgan shrugged. "But when Melissa Roberts came along, she had a whole new set of questions. He fell like a ton of bricks. Then she decided she was too pretty to be stuck up on some windy hill while he was off shoeing horses. One day he came home to an empty house. His pride and his heart both got broken at once. So I guess you can see why I was mad when I first met you, to think he was jumpin' into something too fast."

"I do understand. What about you?" Laura questioned him. "Any ex-wives in your past?"

"Not even a near-miss," he joked. "I guess nobody ever wanted me bad enough to sign papers."

Had she been poked with a cattle prod, she still wouldn't have opened her mouth at that moment. She was afraid of the words she would speak: *I want you.* She didn't want to think it, much less say it. *I want you.*

"And you?" he continued, threading his fingers through

hers as he walked her into the massive living room. ''Is there a Mr. Carey in your past?''

''No time for a husband. I wanted to concentrate on my career. It seems like I never had time for much of anything until I moved to Montana and learned how relaxing life can be!''

''That doesn't surprise me!'' A smile tugged at one side of Morgan's mouth, then spread to his eyes. ''How about other guys? Did you leave a string of broken hearts in Manhattan?''

Alex didn't count, Laura realized. Stacked up against men like Butch and Morgan, Alex suffered by comparison.

''I dated when I had time. But I've always been so involved with my work. And if I didn't have a date on Saturday night, it wasn't the end of the world for me.''

Morgan lit a fire, flooding the room with golden light and welcome warmth. While he prepared coffee, Laura admired old photographs in an album Morgan had brought from the bookshelf.

''There are some pictures of Butch when he started school,'' Morgan pointed out while offering a steaming cup of coffee.

The freckled face in the snapshot squinted at Laura. One hand held a lunch box; the other was lying atop the head of a scruffy dog.

''That's Tuffy. He was heartbroken when Butch started school. He waited at the bus stop every night.''

Each photograph was lovingly captioned with subject and date in small, concise penmanship. Page after page chronicled the Franklins' life, fleshing out Morgan's parents and grandparents as Laura saw them celebrate holidays, brand and doctor new calves, enjoy family get-togethers, and raise two adorable little cowboys. How unlike the sterile, impersonal homelife Laura's mother had produced. There were no family traditions on which Laura had relied.

"Someone put a great deal of time into compiling these scrapbooks," Laura remarked. "Was it your mother?"

Morgan nodded. "She loved tradition. She was a saver. Every snapshot and school paper and play program got put into these scrapbooks. Butch wanted to heave them out years ago, but I wouldn't let him. They're part of our heritage, part of the history of this ranch. I like to feel I can go back through them from time to time."

"I know what you mean," Laura agreed. "When I moved into my place, instead of remodeling the rooms, I wanted things left the way they were when the Ziminskis owned the place. The stained glass in the bay window, the wainscoting in the kitchen. That's what makes it a home to me."

"You're not going to replace the old light fixtures with neon tubes and cover the wood floors with wall-to-wall carpeting?" Morgan laughed cynically.

"I'm going to leave it the way it is. That's the house I fell in love with, and that's the way it's going to stay." Laura was adamant. She rose to take her coffee cup back to the kitchen, noting as she glanced outside the quarter-sized snowflakes drifting silently over the hills.

"Looks like March is coming in like a lion." Morgan stood behind her, and their reflection in the darkened window combined with the falling snow outside.

"We're not going to have any trouble getting back down the road, are we? Will it drift in?" When the words came out, Laura realized her apprehension was not over being stuck overnight with Morgan. Rather, she didn't want to inconvenience him when she knew how hectic calving time could be.

"Let me make another check of the cows, and then we'll see about getting you back down the hill." Morgan's long strides took him to the front hall, where she could hear him pulling on his pacs and getting into his heavy work jacket. "Make yourself at home."

The door let in a gust of cold air, then slammed, signaling Morgan had gone to check livestock.

Laura washed the coffee mugs and rehung them on hooks under the kitchen cupboard. She turned out the overhead light and went back into the living room.

Serenity. It was the first word that came to mind in describing the ambience of the firelit room. How peaceful it felt, how homey. It was missing just one thing, Laura realized, to make it perfect. Morgan. It was his presence. His broad shoulders, bent over the scrapbooks, had made the room comfortable. Seeing his eyes dance as he pointed out his 4-H ribbons. Watching his huge hands delicately exhibit a piece of his grandmother's china. He tugged at Laura's heart.

Girl, she admonished herself, *you've got to quit thinking about him. He's Janelle Harding's guy, not yours. And besides, you don't want to get involved with anybody.*

As the fire's warmth reached into every corner, the old house creaked, comfortably settling in for the night.

The wind changed directions. Snow plastered against the east windows, covering the panes with a feathery whiteness and obscuring the view. In a land where warm chinook winds could melt two feet of snow in a matter of hours, the weather could also turn as rapidly in the other direction. Spring snowstorms hit quickly, leaving people and animals ill-prepared for dealing with the raw elements.

Laura watched the fire until the logs became glowing coals. She piled lengths of fir on the grate, relishing the pungent turpentine-like smell of balsam erupting as the logs caught fire.

"Laura?" Morgan's voice from the hallway aroused her from her reverie.

She ran to the door, sensing the urgency in his voice.

"Can you give me a hand?" He stood before her, holding the smallest, wettest calf she'd ever seen. Its head lay still against Morgan's chest.

"Oh, Morgan! Is it alive?" Laura reached around him to slam the door closed.

"Barely. Grab that towel, will you?" His head motioned toward the cupboard and Laura pulled a towel from its peg. "Rub her body. Get some circulation going in her," Morgan instructed while he gently lowered the creature onto the rag rug in front of the kitchen sink.

The calf raised its head.

"Keep rubbing!" Morgan patted the animal's shoulder, then turned to Laura. "I've got to get her mother up and into the barn. She had a tough time delivering, and she's worn out. As soon as that calf gets warmed, we'll put her with the mama and start her sucking." He was out the door in the next minute, leaving Laura with the newborn calf.

Using every muscle in her back, Laura massaged warmth into the newborn. Five minutes passed, then ten. Still she continued the process which should have been performed by the mother's licking to get the calf's circulation started.

"Come on, darling," she murmured, feeling warmth at last fill the fragile body. The calf kicked lanky legs and positioned itself to stand. Its eyes surveyed Laura skeptically as it struggled to its feet.

"Whoa, take it easy." Laura gathered the calf into her arms and continued rubbing its back. "You're all right, just take it easy. We're going to take you to your mother." She reached on the back of the kitchen chair and pulled one sleeve of her coat on while maintaining her hold on the wobbly calf.

"Maaaaaaa!" The calf bellowed loudly. The noise broke the silence of the farmhouse, startling both the animal itself and Laura. In spite of herself, Laura laughed. She'd never been a nursemaid for a cow before. Another first in her growing list of Montana life experiences, she mused.

She heard Morgan's footsteps as he stomped excess snow from his boots and came through the door.

"How's everybody doing?" His smile encompassed Laura and her charge.

"She's ready for dinner!" Laura laughed. The calf was skittery. In a clumsy escape attempt, its feet slid on the vinyl flooring and sent it gliding toward Morgan. In one graceful motion, he bent and swooped the calf into his arms.

"Maaaaaa!" The animal's cry was belligerent.

He carried the calf with ease while it bawled all the way to the barn. Inside, he deposited it on fresh straw at its mother's feet. The cow began to nose her offspring.

"She'll be fine." Morgan laid one gloved hand on Laura's shoulder. "You did a good job. You've got a gentle touch."

"I've never been a cowgirl before." She liked the feeling that she'd learned something new.

A gust of wind hit the barn door and shrieked through the timbers of the old building. Overhead, shop lights strung the length of the barn flickered.

"Sounds like that wind is really picking up," Laura commented.

Morgan looked solemn. "We don't need that along with the snow. If any more calves decide to come tonight, it could make things tough."

"Do you usually go through calving season without help?" It seemed incomprehensible to Laura that this could be a one-person operation.

"Butch is usually here. It's just that we don't usually start calving quite this early. We knew the risks when he left for Denver last week. He'll be home in a day or so, and I can make it until then. If things get too crazy, Carl Stillman will come up and help me."

The calf had begun to suckle and its legs were already looking substantially stronger.

"Guess we'd better get you home," Morgan suggested. "This wind could blow the road closed if we don't get moving."

They walked toward the house together.

"I'm sorry you have to take me clear down the canyon in this storm," Laura apologized.

Morgan turned in the moonlight. Snow danced around his face and settled on his eyelashes. His glance licked over her face. "Don't be sorry. I've sure enjoyed your company."

For somebody who had always prided himself on being a loner, he wondered why he hated to see the evening end.

He stomped a path in the snow to his truck and opened the passenger door for her. After locking the hubs into four-wheel drive, he climbed into the driver's seat. The engine fired up instantly. The truck rolled forward in the knee-deep snow as they turned in the drive and started toward the main road. Snow pelted the truck from all directions, overtaking the slapping windshield wipers and rendering them nearly useless.

"I've never seen a storm like this. It's like a blizzard." Laura's voice was shaky in the darkened cab. Snow flurries on the ski hill were wonderful and welcome; blinding, blowing snow on a mountain road in the middle of the night was something else.

Morgan attempted to soothe her. "We're okay. It's just March in Montana," he explained. "You'll see another couple of storms like this before springtime is over."

His complete concentration was on driving as Morgan maneuvered the truck through the snow. They were but a short distance from the house. Laura could still see the hallway light shining beacon-like through the snow.

The truck stopped.

"Well, this is as far as we're going tonight," Morgan said complacently. "This road's drifted in."

"What'll we do?" Laura asked.

"Two choices. We can sit out here and freeze"—he turned and tried to reassure her—"or we can go back to the nice warm house and you can stay here tonight."

Chapter Six

Laura angled the edges of her skis sharply and planted her pole in the snow. Shifting her weight, she zigzagged the mogul field with ease and continued down the mountain. A strong, fast skier, she devoured the hill in a flawless run and glided to an abrupt stop at the base near the lift. The crowds were light today. Spring ski season was drawing to a close as the snowpacked base dwindled in ever-increasing temperatures.

"Good run!" Agnes Stillman complimented her as Laura clomped in heavy ski boots up the stairs to the lodge's sun deck.

Laura pulled her goggles and earband off and grinned. "Why do we work for a living when we could ski every day in this beautiful sunshine!" she laughed.

"Maybe to afford the lift ticket?" Agnes suggested sarcastically. She rarely took time off in the middle of the week, but Carl had insisted on watching the store so she could spend the day on the slopes with Laura.

"You know, when I started coming out to ski in Montana six years ago, a season pass cost just about half what it is now," Laura complained. "That's development for you!"

"When Carl and I first moved here twenty years ago," Agnes reminisced, "this ski area wasn't even built! We used to pull each other up the hill at the Flying G with a tractor, and ski down!"

Laura poured coffee from the thermos and passed it to Agnes.

"At the Flying G? Did you know Butch's parents?"

"I knew them well. They were the finest people you'd ever meet. Tom Franklin was a good-looking guy. Looked a lot like Butch. Acted like him too. Always joking and kidding around. He never met a stranger. Ruth—Mrs. Franklin—was a tall, beautiful woman. Quiet. Classy. Morgan favors his mother both in looks and in temperament."

It had been two weeks since Laura had been snowed in at the Franklin ranch. Morgan had led her to the bedroom formerly used by his parents. He had brought her one of his T-shirts to wear, and had furnished an extra quilt from his own bed. Then she'd been left alone to toss and turn the night away.

When morning came, he shoveled the truck free from the snowdrifts and took her home after breakfast. He had been a perfect gentlemen. The kiss in the barn hadn't been reprised. And he hadn't left her mind for more than an hour since she'd last seen him.

"He's quite a guy," Laura agreed.

"But it's Butch you're interested in," Agnes wondered aloud.

"Not romantically."

Agnes looked skeptical. "Haven't you been dating him since the Community Center Christmas party?"

"Not dates. Just spending time with him as a friend. We went to dinner night before last, as a matter of fact. He's just my buddy."

A devious smile crossed Agnes's face. "Would you go out with Morgan if he asked you?"

Laura shrugged her shoulders. "He wouldn't ask. He's seeing Janelle Harding."

Agnes scoffed. "A guy like Morgan wouldn't waste much time on somebody like her."

"He took her to Jim and Becky Trask's party . . ."

"Small potatoes." Agnes snorted.

". . . then he took her home from the party," Laura finished.

"How do you know that means anything? After all, you spent a night at his place and nothing happened. Besides, he's real. She's plastic. Morgan Franklin is way out of Janelle Harding's league. Now you"—Agnes waved her coffee cup at Laura—"*you* and Morgan would make a good pair."

"Ha ha ha," Laura emphasized each syllable. "I like him, but Morgan and I don't agree on things, Agnes. Maybe he thinks I'm too opinionated. Our politics certainly don't mesh. You know Morgan is against the wolf reintroduction, and I'm starting work next week with Paul Caro on a pro-wolf documentary."

"Politics don't have to mesh, as long as you don't argue about them."

Laura shook her head. "I'm not changing my politics for anybody. Besides, I'm not in the market for a man."

"That scarf"—Agnes pointed to Laura's neck—"did you go to the store specifically to buy it?"

Laura thought for a moment. "No, I think it caught my eye one day when I was shopping for shoes."

Agnes smirked. "I rest my case, Your Honor."

Three more runs finished out the afternoon's skiing and relaxed the two women to the point of exhaustion.

"Flip a coin to see who drives home," Laura suggested.

"I'll drive," Agnes offered. "Let's stop at O'Grady's on the way down the canyon. A nice hot cup of coffee would hit the spot."

A solid string of cars leaving the ski area threaded down the canyon. The sun was setting; the temperature was dropping. Patches of deceivingly treacherous black ice coated the highway, catching unsuspecting motorists and sending vehicles into fishtailing skids.

"I'm glad you're driving," Laura complimented her friend. "I'm still learning how to maneuver on icy roads. When I used to fly out here from New York, I usually took the ski bus from the hotel."

"This part of the road is always the first to develop black ice. There's a warm spring around the bend up here that causes this section to ice over. It'll clear off down by the road to the Flying G." Agnes guided the car smoothly, proficiently coaxing the back end into place when it dared to skid momentarily.

As predicted, the Flying G turnoff served as a demarcation line between black ice and snowy roads. Then, several miles down the canyon, the neon sign from O'Grady's Inn flickered garishly through the lightly falling snow.

O'Grady's was the local watering hole, which on any evening held an electric mix of skiers, cowboys, and retirees. During hunting season, the blaze of orange vests in residence was nearly blinding. When ski season ended, the inn would fill with fly fishermen with bragging rights to the area's blue-ribbon trout streams. Summer saw rodeo riders in high-heeled roping boots bellied up to the bar. Ben O'Grady, the inn's original proprietor, had held the title of All-Around Cowboy in the 1940s. Autographed rodeo pictures plastered the walls of the colorful tavern. On Laura's first trip to Montana, she'd been introduced to O'Grady's by her fellow skiers. She'd never forgotten the easy camaraderie and old-fashioned western flavor of the inn, the smell of hot coffee, and the fresh pine smell of sawdust on the dance floor.

"Well, look at this! Somebody call Carl Stillman and tell him not to pay the ransom—his wife has escaped!" The joking came from Clara Chandler, a tough-as-brass waitress with the proverbial heart of gold. "How was skiing?"

"Great!" Agnes shook her hair loose from her ski cap

and turned to Laura. "Clara, this is Laura Carey. She bought the Ziminski place down the canyon."

Clara extended her hand and shook Laura's with enthusiasm. The action was prevalent in Montana women: instead of demurely nodding to acknowledge an introduction, Laura noticed each woman she met had offered a hand in friendship. It was an endearing gesture. Laura returned Clara's greeting.

"Is there a Mr. Carey?" Clara asked openly. Too many years in the bar business had diminished her sense of discretion. She'd find out anyway—she'd might as well be blunt.

Laura laughed and shook her head. "No Mr. Carey."

"Well, don't worry," Clara consoled her. "As pretty as you are, we won't have any trouble finding you a Mr. Carey if you want one." Clara laughed and nudged Agnes conspiratorially.

"Laura's been seeing Butch Franklin," Agnes related to Clara in a stage whisper.

Laura scooted her chair closer to the small round table and glared at Agnes. "He's just a friend."

Clara winked at the women. "He and the Dickerson boys should be in sometime tonight. They took cows to the vets this afternoon and stopped in for coffee. Said they'd see me on their way back," Clara reported.

The women ordered coffee and enjoyed watching the crowd. Nearly every cowboy in the bar tried vainly to catch Laura's eye. The day's exertion had flushed her face with color and added sparkle to her eyes.

"I'm going to call Carl and let him know we've stopped for an hour or so." Agnes slid her chair back and nodded toward the pay phone across the room.

Savoring the liquid warmth of her coffee, Laura emptied her cup and sat back. Skiing had invigorated her. Now the warm room was taking the edge off her energy.

"Hey, Beautiful, how was the skiing?"

Butch burst through the door, looking like an overgrown gingerbread man in his brown canvas overalls and heavy brown pacs.

"Hi, Butch!" Laura smiled with pleasure, mirroring Butch's infectious grin. "Skiing was divine! How was your day?"

"Busy. Took two of our cows up to Doc Hill's."

"How's calving going?"

Butch shook his head in wonder. "We're almost done. Those calves came faster this year than anything I've ever seen. The snow's been dry enough that we haven't had many problems at all. By the way," he added, "thanks for your help. Morgan tells me you took over and saved a calf while I was gone. Thanks for keeping him company."

"One night. Join us for coffee?" Laura scooped her hat and mittens from the chair beside her and pushed it out for Butch.

"Just one cup. I followed the Dickersons down the canyon. They helped me load livestock this morning. They're going up to our place and check cattle tonight for me."

"Where's Morgan?" Laura asked. *On my mind about half the time,* she answered herself.

"He's home. He's been burning the midnight oil all through calving season and I thought he needed a break. The Dickersons said they'd spell us off the next couple of nights so Morgan can relax a little and I can get some things done in town."

Clara reappeared with a full coffeepot and poured a cup for Butch.

"My one and only." Butch laughed, referring to his limit on coffee but flirting nonetheless with the middle-aged Clara.

Butch launched into his repertoire of jokes, to the delight of the two women at his table. Before long, several locals had joined the table and their laughter carried throughout the bar.

Laura felt the rush of cold air as the door opened behind her. Without looking up, she drained her coffee cup. This was fun! It had been a busy month and she relished the relaxation of a day off.

"Well hello, Handsome!" Clara sashayed across the floor to welcome the newcomer. "You'd better come and let your little brother buy you a cup of coffee."

Morgan Franklin hung his black cowboy hat on a peg inside the door and strode casually to their table.

"Sit down, buddy!" Butch slid an empty chair toward his brother, who flopped down and rested his huge hands on the table. He surveyed the group around the table, nodding to each.

Feeling his glance stop at her, Laura blushed but couldn't turn away from him. She knew her hair was a mass of unruly curls from being blown on the ski hill all day. Her face was windburned, heightening the color in her cheeks.

Rats, I should've combed my hair or at least brought some lipstick, she thought.

She boldly returned his unwavering stare.

His gaze broke away first. "Will you please bring me a cup of coffee, and get us another round here, Clara?"

At that moment, the jukebox in the corner came to life with the thump, thump, thumping bass of a country beat.

"Come on, Laura, let's cut a rug!" Butch reached across the table and pulled Laura from her chair. They twirled onto the dance floor and joined the two-stepping crowd in a circular pattern. When the song ended, they rejoined the group.

". . . saw tracks in his pasture last night." One of the ranchers at the table had captured everyone's attention.

"Tracks?" Laura joined the conversation.

"Wolf tracks. Chuck Jensen spotted them in his north pasture."

"From Yellowstone Park?" Laura knew six sets of

breeding pairs had already been released in the past several weeks.

''Undoubtedly. They never should have released them this close to the park line.'' The ranchers murmured in agreement. ''If they go after our livestock, they'll be dead before six months pass.''

''Can't they be recaptured and taken further into the park?'' Laura questioned. Paul Caro had begun footage for his documentary on the wolves, using study center animals from a refuge in Minnesota. Tomorrow after he arrived at the airport, he and Laura would be filming an actual release in Yellowstone Park. She sought reassurance. ''Must they be shot?''

''You brought a new calf to life,'' Morgan reminded her. ''Would you want to see her killed by a wolf?''

''Of course I wouldn't,'' Laura conceded. ''But how would you know for sure she was killed by a wolf and not by one of the dog packs running at night? You know as well as I do that with the subdivisions sprouting farther up the canyon, more and more people are moving in with dogs and letting them run unleashed.''

''That's right.'' Butch nodded in agreement. ''The dogs are becoming a problem.''

''I just think you need to be very sure any livestock losses are due to wolves before you start shooting.'' Laura was adamant.

One of the cowboys, his palm wrapped around a beer can, shook his head disparagingly. ''Anybody who wants wolves back in the park is crazy.''

Laura bristled. ''Because they don't agree with your perspective? I don't think so! I want the wolves, and I'm certainly not crazy.'' She straightened her shoulders and leaned toward the cowboy. Her eyes lost their amused sparkle and were dangerously, coldly bright. Her body language said, *I'm ready for a confrontation if you insist.*

The cowboy sneered. ''What if one ate your livestock?''

"If I were sure it was a wolf-kill, I'd stand watch and shoot the predator," Laura answered confidently. "But not every wolf in the park is crossing the boundaries and coming after livestock. It's a well-managed program and it deserves more credit than you're giving it. Give it some time to work."

The cowboy, disgruntled at being challenged, stood and looked at Laura contemptuously. "You've got a lot to learn about living in Montana. This isn't a western movie. This is real life."

Laura nodded in agreement. "I realize that. But since I moved here, I've heard over and over that people want Montana kept unspoiled and natural. The wolves are part of that natural order. The natural cycle of the Yellowstone ecosystem was here centuries before you or me. It's more real life than either of us will ever see." Her eyes bore through him until he turned and resumed his place at the bar.

"Whew! Russell's not used to women standing up to him!" Agnes laughed. "Good job!"

Morgan sat quietly, watching the exchange between his brother's beautiful girlfriend and the obnoxious cowboy who had a reputation for belligerence.

He couldn't agree with Laura on this issue; he never would. Despite his opinion, he admired the way she had defended her beliefs. She didn't back down from controversy. The woman definitely had fire.

"Dance time!" Butch grabbed Agnes by the hand.

Morgan tapped the rim of his coffee cup with one finger in time to the music.

Laura swallowed hard. "Dance with me, Cowboy?" Her invitation was uncharacteristically, deliberately flirtatious. She had lain awake nights thinking about him. Every ounce of logic warned her to stay away from him. She didn't need the complication of a man in her life. But if she didn't dance with him just this once, if she didn't feel his arms around her for even a few brief minutes, she knew she'd be kicking herself the rest of the week.

Why couldn't he have asked first? Laura fretted. *Maybe he'll say no. Maybe he wishes Janelle were here to dance with him. Maybe . . .*

He rose and took her hand, his eyes never leaving her face. His face betrayed no emotion as he pulled her against the rocklike hardness of his chest.

The after-ski crowd congested the dance floor. An elbow gouged Laura's back and she felt Morgan's arm tighten around her.

"Good music," she murmured against his shoulder.

She felt him nod in agreement.

His hands were hard with calluses. She relished the feeling of his palm marvelously pressed to hers. The song would never be long enough, Laura realized; if it went on forever it wouldn't give her enough time in his arms.

She wanted to hear his voice, feel his breath against her cheek. She could feel his pulse where her face rested against his throat. Slowly, trancelike, she raised her lips to the spot.

Was the music still playing? Laura couldn't say. The world within Morgan's arms was all that existed—all that mattered.

"Hey, Morgan!" A rancher in faded denims danced next to them. "How's calving?"

The spell was broken.

"Going good. Winding down," Morgan responded. "In fact, the Dickersons are taking over for me tonight so I can relax."

The song ended and the crowd disbursed to individual tables or to the bar. While Laura's dance partner excused himself to continue his conversation, she returned to the table, where Butch and Agnes were arguing the merits of a state sales tax. With Montana's high property taxes,

Butch was adamant about the need for tax reform. As a merchant, Agnes was equally firm against it.

"Hate to break up your friendly chat," Laura interjected, "but I've got to get Agnes home before I get in trouble with Carl."

Agnes laughed. "You're right. By now, Jason and his dad will have finished the supper dishes, so it's safe for me to go home!"

Butch stood and held Agnes's jacket, then wound Laura's scarf around her neck and flipped it over her shoulder. His older brother continued talking on the dance floor, glancing up only when he heard Clara's good-bye from across the room.

"You two behave and be careful driving home!" The waitress's voice rang out above the crowd.

Laura let Butch's hand linger on her hair as he arranged her scarf, knowing the scene was not going unnoticed by his brother.

You're so cold, Morgan Franklin, she anguished. *Why can't one dance affect you the way it bothers me? Why must I wake up nights and think about you?*

"I saw what you did when you were dancing." In the comfortable silence of the ride home, Agnes's words came not as an accusation but more as a gentle, surprising revelation.

"Which was?"

"You kissed Morgan. You shut your eyes and kissed him." Agnes was both direct and amused.

Laura sighed. "I couldn't help myself."

"Nothing wrong with that."

"I feel like a fool. Never in my life has anybody mixed me up like he does."

"Sounds like real chemistry to me."

Laura shook her head and watched Agnes maneuver the

car on the icy highway. "He doesn't feel the same. I'm afraid of making a fool of myself."

"What if he does feel the same? Would you still feel foolish?"

"He's got Janelle. He's not interested in me. Besides, I'm too busy for a boyfriend."

With a cross between a laugh and a snort, Agnes disagreed. "Girl, even a one-armed beekeeper isn't *that* busy. Whatever feelings are happening between you two aren't going to wait for you to get over being busy. I saw how you looked at each other tonight. There's definitely something there. Definitely."

"Maybe chemistry isn't everything."

"You're wrong there, girl," Agnes contradicted her. "Do you know that after all these years with Carl Stillman, the man still makes me melt inside? Sometimes I look at him and wonder how anybody can love anything as much as I do that man. Some people never find that kind of love in their whole lifetime. If it comes along, you jump on it. Don't question it, don't analyze it. Just jump like heck on it."

It was dark when they pulled into the parking lot of the Stillmans' store. Carl unloaded his wife's ski equipment while Jason helped a customer pump gas.

"Thanks for loaning me your partner for the day, Carl. I love our ski trips and our heart-to-heart talks!"

"You're a bad influence on her, Laura." Carl laughed as he slammed the trunk of the car. "Two beautiful women like you at O'Grady's with all those lonely cowboys—I'm just lucky she came home to me."

In the rearview mirror, Laura saw the two of them, their arms wound around each other's waists, as she headed down the highway.

That's what love should be, she thought. *It's what marriage could be. And what it is for Agnes and Carl. Will it ever be that way for me?* she wondered.

Chapter Seven

Laura flipped over in bed, punched her pillow, and squinted at the clock. It was well past midnight, yet sleep had eluded her despite the rigorous day of skiing. The image of Morgan's face danced before her.

You've invaded my sleep, Morgan Franklin, but you're not going to invade my heart.

She swung her feet to the floor and pulled her bathrobe around her. The house was cool. Silver ribbons of moonlight draped across the parlor furniture, lending a surrealistic glow to the room.

Laura lit the lamp at the end of the sofa and flicked on the television. She channel-surfed through infomercials and an old comedy series rerun before settling on a classic western. Half an hour into the movie, she realized she was watching John Wayne but her mind was picturing Morgan.

The whine of tires battling the slushy road out front caught her attention. She knelt on the window seat cushion and pulled the curtain aside.

Brake lights glowed in the dark as the truck halted in front of her gate. The driver's door opened. She could see Morgan's cowboy hat silhouetted in the moonlight as he started around the front of the truck toward the house.

Clutching her robe tightly around her, she opened the front door to the crisp night air.

"Morgan?"

She watched him wind his way through the gate and up

the walk. His hat was pushed back on his head, and he grinned when he saw her in the doorway.

''Good evening, Miss Carey.'' He tipped his hat in an exaggerated bow. He ambled loose-hipped into the middle of the parlor. ''Saw your light, hoped you were up.''

He grinned a lopsided smile, a tad mysteriously.

''Sit down while I make coffee. Let me hang this up for you,'' she offered. He shrugged out of his sheepskin jacket and made himself at home on the sofa. While she measured coffee and started it brewing, she could hear him softly humming a Jimmy Buffett tune.

Her coffee mug forgotten on the end table, she paced between her chair and the fireplace. Crumpled newsprint and a pyramid of logs, stacked like a funeral pyre, lay waiting to be lit. She grabbed a wooden match and savagely struck it against the hearth mortar. It flared to life. The flames erupted beneath the logs and sent shimmering lights across her face, now contorted with worry. Every nerve was taut as she turned to face her guest.

''Do you want to talk about it?''

''Yep.''

The clock ticked.

Outdoors, melting snow on the porch roof dripped down with a steady *splat, splat, splat.*

The coffeemaker hissed in the kitchen.

''Well?'' Laura's patience was fleeing quicker than chimney smoke.

''I've done something real stupid.'' A grin stretched across his face. Black curls crawled over his collar and bade Laura to comb them with her fingers. She denied herself the luxury of touching him. His usual somber, hard-jawed demeanor had been replaced by a reckless, casual charm Laura tried to ignore.

''Which is?'' she prompted him.

His eyes focused on her. The grin disappeared.

"I'm afraid"—his voice was low—"I've fallen in love with my brother's girlfriend."

A hundred thoughts bombarded Laura's mind at once. *What brother . . . doesn't he have just one? Who's Butch's girlfriend? How come I haven't met her? Or—wait a minute—does he mean . . . ?*

He shook his head. "It's a real mess. I know Butch saw you first, but I love you."

"Morgan, have you been drinking something stronger than coffee?"

He looked her straight in the eye. "Absolutely not. If a man has to have alcohol to bolster his courage, I don't figure he's much of a man."

"I'm glad you feel that way."

"I love you, Laura. I think I've loved you since the first time I saw you, standing right there in that doorway." He pointed toward the bedroom.

Her knees shook. Were he wearing a hockey mask and carrying a chainsaw, he couldn't have frightened her more.

"Answer me one thing," he implored her. "Are you in love with Butch?"

She found her voice at last. "I told you before and I'm telling you now. Butch is my friend. Nothing more. Not now, not ever. He knows that, and it's high time you know it."

Relief washed across the cowboy's face. "I only know I love you."

"Darn it, Morgan. You come here in the middle of the night and tell me you love me? You don't even know what you're saying!"

"I'm saying I love you."

Visions of the Trasks' party and Janelle Harding danced across her mind. *Well, Morgan Franklin,* Laura thought furiously, *the moon is not full tonight and I am not Janelle Harding.*

"You looked pretty chummy with Janelle Harding not very long ago."

Morgan breathed an exasperated sigh. "I don't love Janelle, I love *you*. Will you believe me in the noonday sun if I tell you again?"

She couldn't answer. Her emotions were playing havoc with her logic.

"I'll be back." Morgan clutched his jacket with one hand and fit his hat on with the other.

The roar of his truck faded as it headed toward the highway, leaving behind a cozy white frame house and in it, a woman whose tears inexplicably would not stop.

Half a whole-wheat waffle and a glass of orange juice sat untouched on the table. Morning sun bathed the kitchen a lemon yellow while a Beethoven CD thundered the Emperor's Concerto throughout the house.

Beethoven. Morgan. They were inextricably connected in Laura's mind since the night she had spent at the Flying G.

"Quit thinking about him," she admonished herself. Crumbling the uneaten waffle, she threw it out the back door for the birds.

She dressed quickly, checking her watch against the digital readout on the microwave. Paul Caro's flight was arriving at nine this morning, and it was a half-hour drive to Gallatin Field.

Spring had arrived in the valley. The drive to the airport took Laura past farm fields with pinto spots of snow growing ever smaller in the greening grass of springtime in the Rockies. Young calves gamboled in the pastures, waving hello with their flickering tails. Ice gorging on the river had sent huge chunks over the bank into stubble fields, while the freed water surged purposefully on course. At this altitude, the sun radiated heat even this early in the year.

Incoming flights were being announced as Laura ran through the revolving door of the airport. She rushed to Gate 3 and awaited the arrival of the famed videographer. Minutes later the plane touched down and taxied to the jetway.

"Paul!" Laura waved and caught the deplaning passenger's attention as he exited the jetway. He smiled, his travel-weary face shedding its look of serious concentration. His thick, graying hair was pulled into a ponytail and he wore khakis and loafers. Camera bags dangled from both shoulders; these he would never trust to the baggage compartment. He shouldered his way through the crowd and took Laura's hand.

"How good to see you again, Laura." His voice betrayed a touch of East Coast accent that Laura found oddly discordant after being away from it for these past months.

"Did you have a good flight?"

"Fine. Fine." Organized to the nth degree, he pulled a small spiral notebook from one of the numerous pockets in his vest and flipped it open. "I show we're meeting the Park Service people at noon. Is that still on?"

Laura nodded. "We'll meet them at the ranger station and follow them to the acclimation pens. The release is set for one o'clock this afternoon."

His bag was retrieved from the revolving luggage carousel and the two headed to the parking lot.

"You're traveling light," Laura noticed.

Paul grinned. "One down vest, a couple of wool sweaters, and some blue jeans. Isn't that standard fare for this area?"

Laura glanced down at her similar clothing. "Perfect." She laughed.

After stowing the bag in the trunk, she buckled into the driver's seat and unfolded the map of Yellowstone Park.

"This is the route we're taking. We're just a couple of

hours' drive from the West Yellowstone entrance to the park.''

''So tell me, Laura, how do you like being a Montana woman?'' Paul's arm rested comfortably on the back of the seat as Laura turned onto the highway.

Her smile told it all. ''I love it, Paul. Although I really can't be considered a Montana woman yet. Around these parts, if your family hasn't lived here fifty years, you're considered a newcomer. But I do enjoy it. This is how life should be lived! My little acreage is like heaven on earth.''

''You don't miss the excitement of New York?''

She shook her head. ''Not at all. I've never been bored a moment since I moved here. The people are wonderful.''

''You look great. This country living must agree with you,'' he remarked. Laura's enthusiasm for life had impressed him the first time he talked to her on the phone. She was bright and ambitious. He admired her chutzpah in following her dream.

Laura concentrated as she swung past a truck towing a horse trailer, then continued toward the canyon.

''You know,'' she reflected, ''it took me a little while to feel comfortable in the community. But now I've made some really good friends.''

''You're here to stay, then?''

''I'll always travel, Paul, but this is home. As crazy as it sounds, I feel like this is what I've been looking for. I want to spend the rest of my life in this place.''

''Alone?'' His eyes narrowed as they skimmed Laura's features.

Her laugh was too short, coming too fast. It sounded cynical.

''You show me the man worth giving up my independence for, giving up everything I'm working toward''— Laura's eyes blazed as she smiled smugly at Paul—''and I'll recommend him for sainthood. But,'' she added, ''I won't marry him!''

* * *

The late-afternoon sun, glistening golden across the crusty, melting snowdrifts, fragmented the forest into corduroy stripes of light and shadow as Paul unpacked his photographic equipment.

"You can set up here," the wolf biologist motioned to them.

The knoll, sheltered by lofty pine trees, overlooked the release site and provided a vantage point for their cameras while affording some degree of camouflage.

Three wolf packs, each consisting of an adult breeding pair and their pups, roamed the one-acre holding pen within the boundaries of Yellowstone Park. The four pups belonging to the alpha, or dominant, pair were approaching nine months old and exhibiting their assertiveness. Grunting and puffing, they tugged competitively at a deer carcass furnished by park personnel.

"Now remember," the scientist cautioned them, "wolves don't like people. They'll avoid this area because of the equipment and because you're here. It may be minutes, or possibly even hours, before they'll leave the enclosure."

Paul nodded in understanding. He tightened his tripod joints and set a camera atop it. A still camera was positioned on a second holder. Paul hoisted a video camera onto his shoulder. Laura followed suit with a third camera into which she had clicked a video magazine.

The alpha female, exhibiting unusual curiosity and boldness, padded along the perimeter of the pen toward them. Her eyes, gleaming yellow like molten gold, swept over Paul and Laura with fierce intensity. Laura returned her stare, too fascinated to turn away.

Wild, furious energy sparked from every fiber of the huge wolf. Her coarse, thick coat rippled with each slow, deliberate step. With ears pricked in vigilance, she tilted her head to catch any foreign sound. The scruff of her neck fanned as she sniffed the air cautiously.

Laura's fingers were numb with cold: a combination of frigid, high-mountain air and the excitement of the project. A sense of awe surrounded her as she observed the wolf.

Powerful forelegs carried the animal past the cameras' viewfinders. The only sound was the soft whir as frame after frame captured the proud, powerful creature's movement. Her paws flexed loosely as her gait increased into a lope across the pen. She approached her pack. Her influence over the group was obvious. Other females and lesser males postured in submission as she returned to them.

The pen doors opened. The rasp of metal connecting rings echoed across the pen as the barriers were eliminated.

Five minutes went by, then ten.

The wolves grew restless; their ears perked, their muscles tensed. Two of the pups tugging at the carcass released it simultaneously and sought direction from the pack's leader.

All cameras focused on the alpha male as he began purposefully striding toward the pen opening. He investigated the gate threshold, as if trying to reason the significance of the barrier being removed. Behind him, the pack awaited his direction.

The wolf's heavily muscled shoulders quivered with anticipation. His body thrust forward, loping nervously in a circular pattern around the pen. On the second lap, he broke into a run. His stride increased in length until his body looked airborne. His pen-mates followed suit, their thickly fluffed tails gracefully undulating behind them. The parameters imposed by the acclimation pen dissolved as the alpha male fled its confines. Following suit, the other wolves bolted.

The three packs bound toward the forest's edge, never breaking stride as verdant fir trees enveloped them. Within minutes, they were gone from sight.

A whisper of a breeze sent snow fluttering from treetops

as it rustled pinecone-laden limbs. All that remained within camera range were wolf tracks in the snow.

Laura tried to find words adequate for what she had just experienced. The wolves' beauty and instinctive power were overwhelming. How could anyone be a spectator to such an event and fail to be moved?

"Quite a sight, wasn't it?" Paul's voice was hushed.

"Completely amazing," Laura murmured.

Paul pulled the camera from his shoulder and laid it gingerly in its case. "Did it frighten you when the female came so close to the fence?"

Laura shook her head. "It's remarkable. I didn't feel any sense of fear. I was just so enthralled by her power. She was absolutely majestic!"

Paul agreed. "The group dynamics fascinated me. Did you see how much control she had over that pack? They clearly took their direction from her."

"All except the big alpha male." Laura laughed. "He's going to have a job keeping her in line. It looks like she can handle herself."

"Poor guy." Paul laughed. "And to think they mate for life!"

"I can't wait to preview our footage." In Laura's mind, she had already begun cutting scenes for the documentary.

The temperature was dropping in direct proportion to the rate of sunset. By the time the equipment was loaded, frost crystals ballooned with each person's breath. Returning to the ranger station, Laura and Paul warmed in front of the blazing wood stove. Eager to hear the specifics of the documentary, the park personnel kept them plied with questions. It was nearly midnight by the time Paul had thanked the crew and collected model release forms from each person appearing on film.

Night wrapped the ranger station in a cocoon of darkness as the two set off down the narrow road winding through the trees toward the park boundary and on into

West Yellowstone. The stillness of the park was replaced with the drone of snowmobiles on the streets of the small town, famous for its record snowfalls each winter.

Over dinner at a rustic lodge on the edge of town, Paul and Laura compared notes on the filming and did some preliminary planning.

"We've got less than twelve weeks from today to have a finished product to public television," Paul reminded his editor. "If we put in some hellishly long days this week, we can get enough of it together that I can take a preview tape back to New York with me. I'm meeting next week with the managers of the foundation sponsoring the project."

Laura nodded in agreement. "They'll be pleased," she assured him. "I know we got some spectacular footage today."

"Coupled with the file tapes I already have on the wolves from the study center, plus the interviews, I think we've got everything we need." Both knew the voluminous stacks of tape necessary to pare down to a one-hour broadcast presentation.

"This has got to be one of the most exciting projects I've worked on." Laura's face flushed with eagerness. "I can't wait to get home and start editing."

The exhilaration of the day, coupled with the altitude to which he was unaccustomed, lulled Paul into a catnap as Laura drove home. She watched the road carefully, mindful of wildlife attempting to cross at this time of the night.

Her headlights caught the luminescence from the ski area sign, glaringly bright in the stygian darkness of the canyon. Farther down the highway, the lights from O'Grady's Inn were mirrored on the tops of vehicles in the parking lot. The road was deserted tonight. Too late for tourists, too early for people leaving the inn.

The Flying G Ranch sign loomed in the periphery of

her lights as Laura passed the arterial road to the Franklins'.

Morgan Franklin's image flashed into her mind. In the quiet of the car, in the dark, he filled her thoughts with agonizing clarity. Less than twenty-four hours ago, he had professed his love for her.

He didn't know what he was saying. They hadn't known each other long enough. Moreover, did she want to believe him?

Clenching the steering wheel to control the quivering of her hands, she took a deep breath and pressed her lips tightly together. She wouldn't let herself be fooled by words of love. Her work was her life now. Besides, she most certainly did not love Morgan Franklin.

Like? Very much so.

Interest? Undoubtedly.

But love? No . . . no. *No!*

Her fingers beat out each category on the wheel as she drove. The soft thump, thump, thump they made as she counted off was eclipsed only by Paul's soft, labored breathing as he slept, and by the deeper, stronger beat of her heart as she pictured Morgan's smile.

Stars punctuated the ebony sky as Laura turned off the highway and drove toward her house. The spring thaw had softened the road into a claylike mud. The car swayed as it caught in ruts left by wider vehicles and by four-wheel-drive trucks on the farm road.

She rolled the window down, letting the refreshing spring air fill the car. This near the mountains, it was still cold but lacked the frosty bite it had held in the park.

Paul stirred next to her, blinked, and sat up.

"Whoa," he muttered. "I must've dozed off."

"This thin mountain air catches quite a few visitors." Laura laughed. "I let you sleep. You're two hours ahead of us on Eastern Standard Time, so right now your internal body clock thinks it's four in the morning!"

Paul reached for his watch and pressed the lighted dial function to confirm the time.

"Did I sleep all the way from West Yellowstone?" he asked, incredulous.

"Every mile."

"I suffer from continual jet lag. It's hard to believe I slept so soundly and can awake so refreshed. Say, this road is a little choppy." He watched the headlights bounce ahead in the burrowed road.

"Spring breakup. My neighbors warned me when I moved in that the spring thaw would make this road almost impassable for a day or so. With the money I make on the wolf project, I'm going to invest in a four-wheel-drive truck. It's almost a must out here."

In the dim lights of the dashboard, Paul glanced at Laura and marveled again at her determination.

"One more hill and we're home." Laura nodded ahead and sighed. "Even in the dark, I love this drive."

The front gate screeched in the still night air as they hipped through with armloads of equipment. The yellow glow of the porch light sprang to life as Laura flicked the switch to illuminate the front walk.

"Looks like I've had a visitor." She nodded toward the front door, where a piece of paper secured with duct tape fluttered for attention.

She pulled at the bottom of the page and stood in the open doorway, twisting the paper toward the light.

I was here in the bright noonday sun, it read, *to tell you I love you. See you tomorrow.*

Her shaking hands rattled the paper as she tossed it on the table near the door.

"Everything okay?" Paul saw the color drain from his friend's lips.

"Fine." Laura's voice sounded far away. But she would have argued with anyone rather than admit that at that moment, her thoughts, as well as her heart, were up the canyon at the Flying G Ranch.

Chapter Eight

A choir of meadowlarks signaled the approach of dawn, and within minutes the horizon was streaked in burning shades of orange as morning broke over the Gallatin Valley. The lowing of cattle from Jensen's neighboring pasture carried on the early-morning breeze. Laura sat on the back porch in her sweat suit, sipping cocoa and curling her toes underneath her in defense from the cool air.

Anticipation knotted her stomach. Excitement at starting the edits, coupled with the anxiety of rereading Morgan's note, had taken its toll on her sleep.

The guest room door had been closed when Laura awoke. Paul was taking advantage of the country quiet to catch up on his sleep.

She looked out toward the mountains. Blackrock Peak loomed highest in the range, solemn and formidable. Above the timberline, snow lay solid on the apron of the mountain, shining purple in the distorting light of dawn. Colorful wildflowers had obstinately begun to encroach on the snow. Bluebells and crocuses splashed color down the mountainside.

A doe picked its way across the muddy meadow. Maintaining a safe distance from the house, it stared at Laura with huge, unblinking eyes.

"Hello, beauty," she crooned softly.

The deer stood transfixed another minute before turning

and flashing its white tail. It bounded across the greening grass and disappeared into the willows bordering the creek.

A fat robin fluttered to the fencepost and perched, head cocked, inspecting Laura. After a few moments' stare-down, it flew to the ground and listened for worms. Finding its reward, it bobbed twice, pulling the rubbery feast from the dirt.

Go build your nest, Laura thought as the robin swooped across the yard toward the beginnings of a straw-and-twig clump in a nearby cottonwood tree.

Spring was such a season of renewal, she realized. The doe was swollen wide with a fawn. Before long, the robins would have their eggs; life reaffirmed. Generations continued. Last week, Agnes Stillman had mentioned looking forward to grandchildren someday. Fifteen years from now, Agnes would still have family. The love would flourish.

What will I have in fifteen years, Laura asked herself. *A room full of videotapes? A mortgage-free homestead with my own shadow for company? Fifteen more years of proving I don't need anybody?*

What else? she thought almost desperately. *What will I be looking forward to, while Agnes and Carl spoil Jason's children and grow old together? Will my film projects be enough to fill the corners of this place? Where will Morgan be in fifteen years?* That worried her the most. Would he be raising little cowgirls and cowboys with his wife . . . with someone not afraid of marriage? She looked out at the vast expanse of the west pasture and shivered.

It was time to start editing. And, she reflected, it was time to stop this silliness. To quit thinking about babies and Morgan Franklin and fifteen years from now. This was here, this was now, and anything else was too unnerving to contemplate.

* * *

The hum of the editing board and click of dials occupied Laura's world for the next several hours. She switched from one tape to another, pulling close-ups of the alpha female wolf into view. On film, the powerful creature lost none of its intensity; it glared menacingly into the camera.

When the phone rang, its peal startled Laura and broke her concentration.

''Hello?''

''Good morning.'' Morgan's deep voice rippled over the wire.

''Good morning.'' *Think of something clever to say,* Laura panicked. ''How . . . how are you?''

She heard his low chuckle. ''I'm in love. How are you?''

The line was silent. Laura could feel her heart beating in her throat.

''I'm doing well,'' she responded, mustering all the coolness her burning lips were capable of delivering.

''Can I come see you?''

Laura ran a hand through her loosely braided hair and glanced down at her faded sweat suit. ''When?''

''When do you want me?''

Twenty-four hours a day, Laura answered silently. *On days that end in ''y''. Every week, every month, every year.*

She glanced at her watch. It was nearly eleven. Paul was still asleep, so there was no need to fix breakfast.

''Come for lunch?'' She was breathless. Hating him for making her feel so foolishly vulnerable, she hated herself more for letting him affect her that way.

''Would you like me to bring anything?'' Why did a simple question sound so suggestive when he asked it? Laura wondered. His voice held a sexy huskiness, tempered with a hint of shyness.

''Thanks, no. I'm in the middle of a project, so it won't be anything fancy. Maybe just a salad and bagels.''

''Sounds great. See you around noon . . .''

She was about to hang up.

''. . . when the sun is shining brighter than a full moon,'' he added. Laura detected the grin in his voice.

This had to be nipped in the bud. Interrupting her work, sabotaging her thoughts, complicating her life. Enough!

She returned to the editing board and resumed working. Skimming through the tape, she prided herself on her perception in choosing the right footage from the myriad of images.

Footsteps in the hallway announced Paul, freshly showered and shaved. He glanced out the front window, admiring the view.

''It's not hard to see what keeps you here,'' he complimented. ''It's beautiful country.''

She smiled in agreement.

''Beautiful and very rugged. Just like the people who live here,'' she added.

''What makes them rugged?''

''Most of the people in this area are old-line ranch families who've been here for generations. They've weathered harsh winters, scorching summers, high property taxes, and low cattle prices just to keep what's theirs.'' She realized she was repeating what Morgan had told her the night she spent at the Flying G. Not satisfied with occupying her thoughts, he now occupied her words as well!

''Admirable loyalty to the land,'' Paul remarked.

Laura nodded in agreement. ''I invited one of the locals to join us for lunch today. His name is Morgan Franklin, and he ranches up the canyon.''

''A rancher, eh? I'll be anxious to talk to him about the wolf issue.''

Laura flinched. ''You may be sorry if you do. As a stockman, he's opposed to the reintroduction program.''

''Life would be boring if everyone agreed on all subjects," Paul philosophized. "It would be great to get some footage from both points of view. Think he'd be willing to be taped?"

Shrugging, Laura suggested, "Maybe. Ask him." To herself, she doubted that Morgan would appear on camera. He was such a private man.

Laura defrosted a bag of frozen bagels and a container of homemade vegetable soup. She spread flowered place-mats on the table, then pulled them up and replaced them with a woven set.

"Don't fuss for me," Paul offered. "I'm so used to restaurant fare that anything will be great. I really appreciate your hospitality."

Fuss for him? She had nearly forgotten Paul's existence, so intent was she on making everything comfortable—perfect—for Morgan's visit.

Paul noticed three place settings on the table.

"He's not bringing his family?"

"Morgan's single." Laura's voice was outwardly calm, belying the fluttering in her stomach when she thought of him.

"Single?" Once Paul spoke the word, it hung in the kitchen, hovering above the dishes and the vase of pine boughs Laura had arranged as a centerpiece. Being deliberately obtuse, he added, "And how does one meet single men in this part of the country?"

"Actually, I dated his brother Butch, whom I met at the community Christmas party. Butch introduced me to Morgan."

"And now it's Morgan who's coming for lunch." Paul's statement held a touch of amusement. He glanced at Laura. The flush in her cheeks told him more than her words said. Paul readily deciphered Laura's vain attempt to appear nonchalant. There were feelings here, he realized, she didn't want to reveal; perhaps not even to herself.

"I'll organize my film logs while we await Mr. Franklin.'' Paul volunteered to give Laura some privacy. ''Call me when your guest arrives.''

The rattle of his truck fenders over the rutted unpaved road announced Morgan's arrival moments before Laura saw the pickup truck pull to a halt in front of the gate.

His long legs unfolded from the cab and he swung the door shut with a firm slam before sauntering around the hood and starting in the gate. His jeans were tight and long. They crumpled slightly to accommodate the instep of his boots. The plaid flannel shirt stretched across his shoulders was tucked in at his narrow waist. The sleeves, rolled up to below his elbows, displayed his rugged, already-tanned arms in sinewy glory. She could see the V of his white T-shirt peeking from beneath the flannel, and above it his determined jaw. His eyes, even bluer than she remembered, danced in his sun-darkened face as he glanced up and saw her in the doorway.

''Howdy!'' He doffed his cowboy hat. A lopsided grin tugged at his lips.

''Come in.'' Laura stepped aside as he took the two stairs in one stride and stood beside her.

He was too tall, too close, too appealing, Laura realized. He was even more dangerous in sunshine than when the moon was full.

''Butch is coming over in about an hour, if you don't mind.'' His eyes never left her face.

''That'll be great. I had a message from him on the answering machine last night but it was late when I got home.''

The doorway was too crowded for comfort, with Morgan's shoulders taking up most of the available space and Laura pressing her back against the door frame to prevent brushing against his body. The cowboy filled the parlor with his presence.

Laura watched him hang his hat on the peg next to the

door, a comfortable, familiar gesture she found oddly satisfying.

"Are you hungry?"

He devoured her with his eyes. "Starving. Something smells good. Have you been baking?"

"I've been editing scenes all morning. You're smelling defrosted bagels." She motioned to the wooden kitchen chair and reached to fill a coffee mug for him. "You're through with calving now?"

"Yep."

"How'd it go?"

"Great! Never lost a calf this season. This is the best bunch we've ever had, I think. Maybe you're the reason for my good luck."

"I doubt that."

"The night you rubbed life into that calf, it wouldn't have survived without you."

Laura beamed. "I loved being there to help."

"That's another of the reasons I fell in love with you." Morgan reached for her hand across the kitchen table and held it gently.

"Morgan, we've got to talk about this. How can you love me when we've only known each other—how many— four months?"

"I fell for you the first time I saw you, Laura. It's hard to believe, I know. It was for me. I didn't believe it was possible, but I can't deny what I felt. I fought it because I thought you were Butch's girl. But I never quit feeling it." His voice resonated in the stillness of the kitchen. "It bothers me to admit it. I didn't ever want to be so far gone on a woman that it interferes with my work. But I think about you all the time, no matter what I'm doing."

Laura was silent. It was one thing to dream of being in his arms. To actually have him sitting there in front of her professing his love was another.

"I guess the next question," he continued, "is how do you feel about me?"

Laura heard a quick intake of breath and realized it was hers. "I . . . am"—she chose her words carefully—"intensely attracted to you, Morgan. There's a strong physical attraction . . . chemistry. There's no doubt about that. But then," she tried unsuccessfully to joke, "maybe I'm just going through a phase. After all, I haven't had a boyfriend for a long time." Her brittle laughter sounded tinny even to her own ears.

Morgan pushed back his chair and stood up. He circled the table and stood behind her, his arms traveling slowly, lovingly from her shoulders to her wrists. Bending to whisper in her ear, she caught his words: "I want to change that."

The beep of the microwave heralded the soup's boiling point. *And mine,* Laura thought ironically.

She took out the soup with oven mitts and placed it on the table, and set out a salad and a plate of bagels.

"Paul, lunch is served!" she called down the hall.

"Paul?"

"Paul Caro is staying here this week. Remember? I've mentioned him to you before."

"Oh, right. He's the cameraman?"

"A videographer," she corrected him. "We were in Yellowstone all day yesterday taping the release of three more wolf packs."

"That's where you were when I came by yesterday at lunchtime." It was just a simple statement, yet Laura detected the disappointment in Morgan's voice at finding her gone.

The filmmaker was buttoning a chambray shirt as he entered the kitchen. With his graying ponytail, designer jeans, and expensive Italian loafers, he personified what the locals disparagingly called a "dude." She immediately felt protective toward Paul as he and Morgan eyed each other warily.

"Paul, this is Morgan Franklin. Morgan, Paul Caro."

The men shook hands and remained on either side of Laura, sizing each other up.

"Paul is one of the foremost videographers in the world," Laura added by way of explanation. "He shot the Indian Railroad documentary I just finished editing."

"And Laura was the impetus behind the wolf documentary we're working on," Paul added kindly. "The whole concept was hers. She's a genius at story development and editing. If she doesn't win a Burlington nomination for this, I'll miss my guess!"

Lunch progressed as the two men became more at ease with each other. Morgan explained his cattle operation, to Paul's fascination. In turn, Paul described his trip to India and answered Morgan's questions enthusiastically.

As they cleared the table, Paul excused himself to return to the editing room.

"I offered my help. I didn't hear your response," Morgan reminded her.

"Your help?"

"You haven't had a boyfriend in a long time. I haven't got a sweetheart myself. What's the common denominator here?" His voice was low, barely more than a whisper.

She deliberately kept her back to him while she rinsed dishes and filled the dishwasher. What could she say? That she wanted him more, and feared him more, than any man she had ever known? That he held the power to change the life she had worked so hard to make for herself, simply because she loved him?

That was it.

Her hands shook under the running water and her knees knocked against the cupboard door as she admitted it to herself. Oh, no! She was in love with him! Cool, independent Laura Carey had fallen for a cowboy. It was almost funny. So why did she feel tears flowing down her cheeks?

"Laura? I didn't mean to embarrass you, darlin'. Tell me what you're thinking."

"It's crazy, Morgan." She felt his huge hands on her shoulders, turning her around to face him. "I didn't want to fall in love. I came to Montana to work in peace and quiet. I have a business to run. It's important to me. I don't like having my mind messed up thinking of a man day and night." She leaned against his shoulder, relishing his smell of aftershave and woolen flannel. His hands splayed across her back.

"Are you, Laura? Are you thinking of me day and night?"

She could only speak the truth.

"Constantly." Her voice was soft, plaintive. "I see you in everything I do. It's awful. I picture you working on the ranch. I think about you having your morning coffee. I imagine you listening to your favorite Beethoven."

His smile broadened. His cheek lay against the top of her head.

Laura shivered. Loving him so, as she now realized she did, meant trusting him completely. She had never taken the time to love a man. As a businesswoman, as an artist, as a landowner, she could prove her ability to succeed. As a woman giving herself completely in love to Morgan, could she be assured of success? The risk was great. But so were her feelings for the rawboned, gentle giant.

She pulled away from him and crossed the room. "I do understand how you feel. But you have to understand something, too. This is scaring me, Morgan. You know how I like things neat and organized and all scheduled in advance. You've come into my life and messed things up royally. My work has to be my first priority. I never intended for my life to take this turn. The real estate guide I read never told me to come to Montana and fall in love."

"If you had known it was going to happen, would you still have moved to the valley?" He was fascinated by her strong sense of independence. She could be tough.

Her laugh was abrupt. She wrapped her arms around herself defensively. "I'd have run like the devil in the opposite direction."

"So where do we go from here?" Morgan leaned back against the kitchen counter. The ball was in her court.

Silence hung in the kitchen. The creak of the wooden floor signaled Paul's presence in the hallway.

"Morgan, I'd like to talk to you about the wolf recovery project if you have a few minutes."

The tall cowboy pushed away from his stance at the counter and gestured toward the back porch. The screen door slammed. Laura heard the porch benches being dragged across the floor as the men settled into conversation.

She was tidying the braid in her hair before joining the men on the porch, when she heard a car door out in front.

"Anybody home?"

"Butch!" Laura called. "I'm in the kitchen. Come on in!"

He peered around the doorway, conspiratorially. On seeing Laura, his smile broadened. "Where's Morgan?"

"Out on the porch with Paul Caro."

Butch's cowboy boots clacked on the bare floor as he crossed the kitchen and opened the back door.

She heard introductions being made among the men. Before she could move, the three trooped into the kitchen.

"Be right back." Butch gestured toward the front door and disappeared.

"What was that all about?" Laura looked at Morgan inquisitively.

His shrug was exaggerated as a smile spread slowly from his lips to his eyes. "Guess you'll just have to wait and see."

The front door opened. She heard Butch's footsteps. And something else . . .

A steady *tick-tick-tick* accompanied his steps.

"What . . ." Laura started through the kitchen doorway into the parlor.

Butch stood grinning like an idiot. In one hand was a paper bag. In the other, a nylon leash. And at the end of the leash was the sweetest ball of black furry puppy Laura had ever laid eyes on. His sturdy short legs danced up and down like pistons, his claws making tiny ticking noises on the oak floor. When he wagged his tail, which he did furiously when Laura entered the room, his whole back end shook. He looked up at Laura, black button eyes shining above his downy muzzle, and whined softly.

"Nygaard's dog had pups, and I remembered you wanted a German shepherd from Santa. Morgan thought you might give this one a home," Butch suggested.

She crossed the room and scooped up the pup with one motion. The young dog sought the warmth of Laura's body and burrowed its nose into her neck, licking her ear.

"Oh," she crooned, "you're so beautiful." She lay her head against the pup and felt the tiny creature's heart beating rapidly. "And you're a little frightened."

"He was just weaned this week," Morgan volunteered, watching the pup nipping at the thick auburn braid hanging over Laura's shoulder. "He's not used to being away from the litter."

Through misty eyes, Laura looked at the defenseless creature.

Please, Mother, I'll be nine next week. Can't I have a dog for my birthday? Laura was suddenly a child again, remembering.

"Animals belong outdoors, Laura Marie. They're smelly and carry diseases. They'll bite without provocation," Mrs. Carey had warned.

Despite pleading from both Laura and her dad, no pets were allowed at the Carey home.

"So, you want to keep him?" Anticipation saturated Butch's question.

Laura held the puppy away from her and watched his paws scramble to reach her. She smoothed him to her and patted his head. "I want to keep him forever." She laughed softly.

"Good!" Butch wiped his brow in mock relief. He held out the paper bag. "Here's some puppy food and his vet tags and collar. Morgan got his shots yesterday."

Laura turned to Butch's brother. "You had him yesterday?"

"Yep. He was with me when I stopped to see you."

The puppy squirmed and Laura set him on the floor. He raced across the room, his rolly tummy high-centering on the toe of Butch's boot as the pup scampered toward the edge of the area rug. The carpet's tassels proved too tempting as the dog grabbed one and shook his head, tugging at the yarn trimming. He somersaulted, stood on unsteady puppy legs, and fell again. He scrambled to get up and pounced at the base of Laura's wooden rocking chair. Flipping over it, he growled and sank needlelike puppy teeth into the leg of the furniture.

"Come here, sweetie." Laura was on her knees, coaxing the dog back to her. He ran headlong, tripping twice in his haste to return to her.

Paul watched the interaction between his friend and the animal. "I think he's won her over." He laughed.

"Sure. I've been after her love for months, and this little guy just has to walk in the door and trip his way into her heart," Morgan joked. "Now I know where they got the saying 'lucky dog.' "

Laura hugged the pup to her again and kissed his soft, furry head. "Tripper," she murmured softly. "His name is Tripper."

It was long after the men had gone out into the north pasture to tape Morgan's wolf commentary that Laura realized what she had missed earlier that afternoon. It occurred to her only at that moment. Morgan had spoken of her love in front of both Butch and Paul. Maybe they weren't listening as closely as she. Maybe they hadn't picked up on it.

They had.

Paul watched Morgan suspiciously as the videotape captured the elder Franklin's opinions.

Don't lead her on, Cowboy, Paul implored him silently, *if you don't mean it.*

Butch had caught Morgan's remark as well.

Don't break his heart, little Miss New York, was Butch's unspoken plea, *because you have the power to do just that.*

Chapter Nine

"Hey, Jason!" Laura cranked the car window down and yelled at the youngster washing windows at the grocery store. "Come see what I've got!"

"How's it goin', Laura?" he called back, setting aside his bucket of suds and a window squeegee.

The boy was rapidly growing into his feet, Laura realized. He plodded toward the car. His T-shirt, a January birthday present from Laura, sported a howling wolf. It was, his mother had confided, Jason's favorite and one he removed only under protest on wash day.

He bent toward the door, his skinny arms outstretched to the roof of the car. Peering inside, he looked past Laura and squinted at Tripper.

"Hey, how ya' doin', boy?" His face split into a grin.

"Tripper wants to visit you while I grab a few groceries," Laura offered. "Would you mind watching him a minute while I run in?"

"No problem." Jason loved dogs, baseball, and spaghetti, in that order. Baby-sitting Tripper would be a treat for him.

Laura brushed dog hair from her slacks and went into the store, leaving the two bundles of growing energy to confront each other. Jason slapped his thigh and called to the pup, who tumbled and tripped across the asphalt driveway to him.

"Well, there's the new mother!" Agnes Stillman

laughed from behind the store counter. "I heard about your bundle of joy."

"He's a handful," Laura conceded. "In the week I've had him, he's devoured three socks and a knob off one of the kitchen cabinets."

"He's teething." Agnes recognized all the symptoms. Puppies and little boys weren't all that different to raise. They both ate things they shouldn't. They both made messes on the floor. And they both were loving additions to any home.

"He's wonderful! I don't know what I ever did without him!" Laura reached for a box of tea bags. "I'd better restock my supply. I've had company all week and between the two of us, we used almost all my tea."

"Has the photographer gone back to New York?" Agnes had visited with Morgan yesterday. She knew it was hard on him, staying out of Laura's way until Paul's business was done.

"His plane left this morning. He left plenty of work behind for me, though." Laura laughed. "There are so many boxes of tape in the editing room I can hardly get through the door."

Business conducted, the women joined Jason outside, where he and the pup romped in the bright sunshine.

"I love him. Isn't he precious?" Laura looked at the dog with adoring eyes. Her enthusiasm was contagious.

Agnes whooped and laughed at Tripper's antics. Her son led the pup into the field behind the store, where they played tag while the two women watched. "He's all of that. I hope you thanked Morgan properly." She fluttered her eyelashes in mock innocence.

"Agnes!"

"Well, I'll tell you, girl, that man stopped in here yesterday, and I saw the look on his face when he told me about you and the pup. Morgan Franklin is a goner where you're concerned. Whether you know it or not, I can tell you, it's a fact.''

The distant sound of Jason and Tripper's playing caught in the breeze and blended with the beat of Laura's heart. Her gaze swept beyond the field to the majestic purple mountains rimming the valley.

''What would you say if I told you I feel the same way as he does?''

Agnes's voice was emphatic. ''I'd say it's about high time you do something about it.''

''Such as?''

''Well, for starters, tell him what you've told me. Tell him that as much as you love that dog—'' Agnes nodded toward the field where Tripper bounded through the tall grass. ''—you love him more. That'll give him a clue where he stands!''

Where he stood, when Laura pulled up in front of her house, was against the fender of his truck, waiting for her.

''You've been gone all day.'' He attempted to look sullen, but his smile got in the way.

''To the airport, to the post office, to have lunch with Shirley Nygaard and show off Tripper, and to Stillman's store,'' she enumerated. Her face was flushed. Wispy ends of hair strayed from the confines of her braid. Her sweater was blotched with dog hair. She never looked more beautiful to him. ''What are you doing off the ranch at this time of the day?''

''Had to run in to the courthouse and renew the license on my truck.''

''Have time for a cup of coffee?'' She hoped he would. He did.

''I've missed you.'' His eyes followed her around the kitchen while he sat with Tripper on his lap, softly stroking the dog's fur.

''Paul and I got so much done. He took a promo tape

with him on the plane this morning.'' Pride in her accomplishment was evident; she wanted Morgan to be proud of her, too.

''You must've put in some long days.''

Laura nodded. ''Each day was two weeks long.''

''I left you alone so you two could work.''

''I appreciate that.''

''But I missed you,'' he repeated.

Missing him, she realized at that moment, had been like a toothache all week, throbbing day and night and never completely leaving her. She had longed to see the face she loved: the lopsided grin, the brooding look that furrowed his forehead when he concentrated, the way his lips rested against the rim of a coffee mug. She had missed his loose-hipped walk, the feel of his hair where it curled around the collar of his shirt, his deep voice.

''I missed you, too.''

In one swift move, Tripper found himself picked up off the man's lap and gently placed onto the floor. Morgan rose and closed the gap between his chair and the spot where Laura had been standing at the kitchen counter. His arms encircled her, enveloping her in a breath-catching embrace.

His kiss was gentle.

His mouth left hers to skim the softness of her cheek. Across to her temple, then dropping to her earlobe, a trail burned as his mouth nibbled and tasted and savored the sweetness of her skin.

''Laura,'' Morgan said huskily, tightening his grasp on her, ''what are you doing to me?''

''I'm telling you that I love you.''

Tripper whined.

The kitchen clock ticked.

A fly buzzed against the kitchen window screen, then banked left to go explore the pasture.

Frozen in time, the cowboy's blue eyes were unwavering. The intensity of his look was laserlike, wearing at Laura's resolve.

His breath escaped in a measured sigh. Lips that had formerly sought their treasure on Laura's, now pressed tightly together. A look of concentration clenched Morgan's jaw.

"This better mean something to you, lady," he spoke quietly. "I'm not just a dumb cowboy out for a good time. I'm in love with you. But I won't walk out that door in a few months and act like this never happened, like I never fell in love with you. You're something special in my life. If you don't feel the same way, tell me now. Don't invite me into your heart."

Laura squared her shoulders and held up her face for his inspection. Her eyes were serious. Her lips trembled.

"I love you, Morgan. This is a big step for me, too. And," she added, "my invitation stands."

With measured, deliberate steps, Morgan went to the back porch, where he deposited Tripper gently in his basket.

The pup whimpered and tripped over the rim of the bed to follow the tall cowboy.

"Stay, boy." For some reason neither of them understood, the animal obeyed.

Returning to the kitchen, Morgan's hand sought Laura's.

The combination of aftershave and his clean male scent assailed her nostrils and thrilled her.

Laura felt her face growing warm as she turned her face to his and planted a kiss on the end of his nose. It was wonderful, the sense of freedom she felt loving him. He made her happy just looking at him, standing in her kitchen, being part of her life.

"Know what I want?" He had spied her bookcase. "I want to see the scrapbook of when you were a girl. I want to know everything about you from the time you were born until the minute you walked into my life."

The late-afternoon sun glistened across the room as the two sat close together on the couch, laughing at pictures of Laura's first dance recital.

"I look like a stork!" She was chagrined.

"You look like a cute little stork."

"I was so homely."

"You are so beautiful." His whisper hung in the air like a benediction. Was the light in his eyes a refraction of sunlight, or did it come from within him? Laura couldn't say.

They talked about politics.

Morgan told her about his hopes for the future. He turned to her, and held her hand tightly. "Laura, you are my life."

He kissed her gently. Laura's brown eyes opened to see Morgan's, never bluer, watching her.

The aura of love pervading the room was palpable. No other place, Laura realized, would ever hold memories so lovingly as this room, on this afternoon, with this man.

"Thank you." Morgan smiled lazily.

"The pleasure is mine," Laura returned.

"The pleasure is you," he corrected. He drew her head onto his shoulder while his arm protectively surrounded her. Brushing her hair back from her forehead, his hand lingered on her cheek. "You big-city girls sure know how to spend a lazy spring afternoon."

"And how many big-city girls have you spent an afternoon kissing?"

His laugh, buried in her hair, made his shoulders quake. "None with your temper! None with your gorgeous eyes and your spirit. None, until today," he finished.

"Mmmm . . . my spirit?"

"You go from being the perfect companion to a complete spitfire in zero to sixty seconds. Every man dreams of that much spirit in a woman."

"Even Butch Franklin's hard-hearted older brother?" she teased.

"Especially him. That's why it took him so long to fall in love. His standards were set pretty high."

"What were you looking for," Laura quizzed him, "that you think you've found in me?" Her hand held his.

Morgan's brow creased with concentration. "I suspect I wanted somebody who could take care of herself . . . somebody who didn't need to hang on me every minute. Somebody tough enough to handle ranch life, soft enough to handle animals and babies, and smart enough to take care of everything in between. I knew the first time I met you that you were comfortable with yourself, with who you are. I could tell your work was important to you, just like mine is to me. I saw the gentleness in you . . . the determination . . . the ambition. You had the right combination. I just never dreamed"—he grinned—"that it would all come together in such beautiful packaging."

She snuggled against him for another kiss and could feel, rather than see, his contented smile.

"What about you? How come I'm here instead of my brother Butch or any of the other cowboys in the valley who tried to catch your eye?"

Laura chuckled softly. "At first, it was purely physical. You're the best-looking man I've ever met. But when I got to know you, I kept noticing things I like about you. I like the way you don't have to look at the words when you sing hymns in church," she enumerated. "I like that you know when to talk and when to keep your mouth shut. You're honest and hardworking and you have the respect of your neighbors. And," she said with a blush, "I love how you look in tight jeans."

"So what made the difference," Morgan persisted, "between my sitting in your kitchen with a cup of coffee, and sitting on your couch kissing you?"

"Simple. I fell in love with you. Besides, you've got

class. You behave like a gentleman. You didn't try to take advantage of me when we were snowed in at the ranch.''

Morgan shook his head and grinned. ''I wanted to.''

''I think I wanted you to. But you didn't. Some men would've, just because the opportunity was there. You've got high standards and brains. That's a hard combination to beat.''

A ringing announcement of an incoming fax jolted Laura. Morgan had moved to the chair and had fallen asleep watching television. Laura had been reading on the couch and discovered she, too, had dozed off. It was nearly eight o'clock, according to Laura's watch. But in her half-awake haze, she couldn't decide if it was morning or night.

She ran toward the machine in the office. At the same time, she heard Tripper's whimpering from the back porch.

''I'm coming, darling,'' she called to the puppy, and was rewarded with his yelps of happiness at the sound of her voice. She scooped up the furry bundle and opened the back porch door. His tiny legs carried him to the far corner of the yard where he dutifully squatted, then raced back to her.

''Good boy! Want a treat?'' Laura sought out the puppy niblets in the cupboard and rewarded his good behavior.

''Am I a good boy?'' asked a voice from the doorway. ''I'll take a kiss for my treat.'' Morgan's voice was scratchy from sleep, and his hair was fanned in back from being pressed against the chair. He looked like an overgrown ten-year-old.

''You are a very, very good boy,'' she assured him coyly. ''And I'm going to feed you some supper before you head back to the ranch.''

Tripper and Morgan entertained each other in the yard while Laura chopped stir-fry vegetables and set the table. Watching the two out the kitchen window, she was amazed once again at the depth of her feelings for the lean, lanky cowboy. Looking at him made her smile; loving him made her ebullient.

"Dinner's ready," she called over her shoulder as steaming platters of rice and vegetables were placed on the table.

The screen door slammed, and Tripper's claws ticking on the floor heralded his entrance into the kitchen. He skidded to a halt in front of Laura and flopped on his back for a tummy rub.

"Tripper, you're a mutt." She laughed. She nuzzled her face into the scruff of his neck and growled softly. He responded with wet, sloppy puppy kisses.

Morgan turned from washing his hands at the kitchen sink to watch the exchange. Never had he seen a woman's eyes light up over one scruffy pup the way Laura had beamed when she met Tripper. She clearly loved the dog. He prided himself on being part of something that brought her that much joy.

Food was secondary to talk at supper. Did Laura wear braces on her teeth as a youngster to achieve that perfect smile? Did Morgan prefer whole-wheat bread or white? Who did he like best, the Cowboys or the Steelers? How many years had it been since Laura's dad died? Who did Morgan take to his senior prom? What did cattle futures look like? Would the initiative pass for a state sales tax? Did Morgan play tennis? They craved every detail of each other's mind.

Tripper was snoozing, head resting on front paws, when Morgan kissed Laura good-bye at the front gate.

"I'll call you tomorrow and wake you up," he threatened.

Laura shook her head. "I'll be up cutting wolf scenes while you're still snoring. And believe me, I know you do snore! I heard you practicing all afternoon."

"I'll call you." He set his cowboy hat squarely on his

head and tilted his face slightly to accommodate another kiss despite the imposing brim.

He gunned the motor of his truck as he pulled out, and Tripper ran to the screen door and whined.

"Just get used to it, sweets." She cuddled the dog to her chest. "I've got work to do and we don't need a man around all the time slowing us down. He's a nice place to visit, but we don't want to live there. It's just you and me, babe."

Tripper scrambled to get down. He ran to the front gate and whined again.

Laura watched as the truck rattled down the road and disappeared over the ridge of the mountain. He was definitely a nice place to visit.

Chapter Ten

Dust plumes rose from the dry corrals at the Flying G, hanging dismal and gray in the air. The glaring sun robbed the day of color, flooding the ground with white-hot light and illuminating each particle of dirt as it swirled in the wind. Permeating each breath was the brittle, burning smell of animal hair as new calves were herded into the branding area.

Butch Franklin reined his horse into the corral and smoothly dismounted. With spurs jingling and chaps flapping, he sauntered to the calf table and watched the branding team sweep the next animal off its feet and into a prone position.

"Good bunch of calves, Butch." Jim Trask latched the calf table and reached for an inoculation gun.

The younger Franklin nodded in agreement. "We've been lucky this spring."

"I know Morgan has been!"

Butch laughed. "That's for sure! He's so head over heels in love I have to repeat everything twice to get it through his thick skull."

"I thought we might see Laura today." Jim Trask, along with his wife Becky, had run into Laura, both with and without Morgan, several times since their holiday party. They enjoyed her friendly, comfortable way of fitting into the community and were happy to see the developing romance between her and one of their oldest friends.

"She'll be here. She's at her place fixing salads for dinner. We told her to stay away until it's time to feed us, or we'd never get any work out of Morgan!" Butch chuckled. His brother had never before let anything gain more importance than ranch work. Since Laura Carey had come into his life, however, Morgan was a changed man: happy, content, confident.

The banter continued as each new calf was marked with the registered brand of the ranch. Because freeze-dry branding was not recognized by the State of Montana as an acceptable marking technique, electric branding irons stood at the ready.

"Think there'll be a wedding this summer?" Jim was hopeful. Morgan had been a long time looking.

Butch wiped dust from his brow on his shirtsleeve and squinted toward the mountains. "There will be if Morgan has anything to say about it. He's ready. But I get the idea that Laura is dragging her feet."

"Why's that?"

Untangling a calf from the head catch, Butch uprighted the calf table and slapped the critter's rump, sending it galloping toward the pens.

"Darned if I know. Some women can't get a ring in a guy's nose fast enough." Butch's chauvinism glared. "Laura isn't one of those women."

Calves bawled for their mothers, who in turn bellowed back at them. Ranch hands kept track of what medicines were dispensed. Ear tags were checked and records maintained. Young bulls were docked. It was hot, heavy work, and by late afternoon, the flare of tempers matched the glare of the sun.

"When I get done here," Butch promised anyone within earshot, "I'm going to drink enough beer to float this whole herd."

"You're going to eat a decent meal first," Morgan warned him as he entered the corral. "The women have got dinner going at the house. We're within about twenty head of finishing.''

At last the instruments were cleaned, calves were safely penned, and the books were closed on another year's branding. Dusty, bone-weary helpers gathered at the two outdoor pumps and rinsed away a day's worth of sweat and dirt. Like fishermen telling about the one that got away, each retelling of the cattle roundup expanded the adventure's lore.

The sun had sunk far enough in the western sky to afford cooling shade. Groups of tired workers dotted the farmyard, balancing platefuls of food on their laps. The stories of past years' brandings reached epic proportions.

Morgan slipped into his room and changed into a fresh shirt before making his way through the crowd in the dining room. Neighbor women had turned the long oak table, his Grandmother Gerard's pride and joy, into a veritable smorgasbord. The rattle of dishes and the smell of casseroles, salads, and strong coffee signaled the end of branding day. The familiarity of the event touched the heart of the man so bent on tradition. His grandparents had celebrated the end of branding with a party; his parents had continued the ritual. He and Butch looked forward to it each year. And, Morgan fervently hoped, someday his children would carry on the custom.

He edged forward in line, taking a plate from the stack at the end of the table, and reached for eating utensils conveniently rolled in a paper napkin. At the same time, he glanced up and saw Laura coming from the kitchen, clutching a roaster full of fried chicken between two oven mitts.

His grin matched hers. She positioned the roaster on the table, her eyes never leaving his face.

''Hi, good-lookin'.'' He wore his heart on his sleeve, to the amazement of the branding crew, who'd never seen this side of the rugged, solemn cowboy.

"Hey, Morgan! Quit tryin' to make time with the cook and get the line moving!" One of the wranglers behind him hollered and caught everyone's attention.

"She's sweeter than any of these pies," Morgan insisted, "and well worth my time!"

His remark was greeted with laughter and hoots of encouragement. Far from being embarrassed, Laura caught the contagious gaiety of the group and realized they had accepted her as one of them.

Pounds of chicken, seemingly acres of salads, gallons of coffee, and dozens of pies were devoured by the cowboys and guests. Afterward, Laura joined Becky Trask, Agnes Stillman, and other neighboring ranch wives to clean the kitchen and distribute dishes to the appropriate donor.

"We fed a real crew today," Agnes remarked as she wiped the kitchen counter clean and rinsed the sink one last time.

Becky paused from sweeping the kitchen floor to nod at Laura. "This poor girl has just passed her initiation. There's nothing like sticking the new kid on the block right in the middle of feeding a branding crew!"

Laura grinned and pantomimed wiping sweat from her brow while the others laughed conspiratorially. It had been a fun day for all.

"Listen . . ." Agnes cocked her head to one side and motioned toward the back pasture.

The sound of a lone violin, clear and light, wafted on the gentle breeze and floated through the open kitchen window.

"Charlie Barnes brought his fiddle." Becky's face brightened. Memories of being courted thirty years ago by that handsome young Jim Trask at another branding party flooded her consciousness. "I was hoping his arthritis wouldn't get him down. It wouldn't be a branding party without Charlie's tunes."

When the kitchen lights were extinguished the women joined the crowd already gathered in the pasture. Lanterns perched on hay bales dotted the darkness and lent an air of magic to the evening.

Two cowboys were unlatching guitar cases and another had retrieved a harmonica from his truck and began blowing a lilting ballad.

Firewood had been stacked in a clearing in the pasture. Tended by a teenaged cowboy in impossibly tight jeans, it awaited lighting. He peered from under the brim of his low-slung hat, hoping the young girls in the crowd would notice his resemblance to Dwight Yoakum.

Laura noticed him, only because she wondered how anybody could bend their knees in pants that constrictive.

He noticed her noticing him, and strutted toward her. Every John Wayne movie he'd ever seen was called into play as his shoulders rotated with each step.

"I hope you save me a dance, ma'am." His cocky attitude was laughable, but Laura realized the importance to boys that age of saving face.

Honey, I've got sweatsocks older than you, she thought to herself. But she smiled at the youth and nodded. "Sure."

He raised two fingers to the brim of his hat in salute, and returned to his designated spot as fire tender.

Laura cruised the crowd, mingling with Jim Trask, Carl Stillman, and a group of cowboys arguing politics and cussing land developers.

Her shoulders were captured in broad hands, and she turned to see Butch Franklin's grinning face. His eyes glazed a little too brightly in the dim light of the lanterns. He smelled like a brewery.

"Hey, buddy, you've been celebrating." She laughed and slid her arm around his waist.

"I'm going to celebrate some more, too," Butch enunciated too clearly, too measured. Laura had seen enough drinkers in her life to recognize Butch's symptoms.

"Be careful," she warned him.

His arm tightened around her waist and he brought his face into close range and leered at the woman in his arms.

"I'm always careful," he whispered gruffly. His head tipped back and he laughed heartily. "But all that could change, huh, Laura girl?" Butch's steps were unsteady, and he rocked back on his heels.

"You'd better sit down, Butch." She helped him to a bale of hay and sat him down.

"We should've fallen in love, Laura," Butch slurred. His eyes focused on Laura, briefly. The effect of too much beer was apparent. "I'd really like to be in love. Why did we just get to be such good friends? I love you, but I don't love you that way. Ya know what I mean?"

"I know, Butch. I love you, too, but not in that way."

"But Morgan," Butch remembered, "now, Morgan you love in that way."

Laura nodded and grinned. "Yep, I do. That way."

Two denim-clad cowboys wandered by and watched enviously as Butch was ministered to by the tall, pretty woman whom they knew to be a New York transplant.

"Joey, Max, meet Laura Carey," Butch called to them.

Both men removed their hats and shook hands with the woman.

"You live around here?" she asked each in turn.

"I'm with my folks on the Bear Creek Ranch," Joe Milliron explained. His years on the family ranch had made him uncomfortable around strangers, particularly pretty women. He shifted from one foot to the other, all the while scuffing into the dirt with the toe of his boot. His shyness was obvious, and endearing, to Laura.

Max held Laura's hand a minute too long. "I work for Gus Higgins over on the Crystal River spread, and ride the rodeo circuit in the summer. And you"—he pointed

to Laura after she had withdrawn her hand from his—
"you bought the Ziminski place, right?"

"Right. Now it's the Carey place," she answered.

"You Morgan's girl?" Max asked without preamble.
He was clearly interested. If she wasn't already spoken for,
he'd welcome a chance to squire her around.

"She is." Morgan's voice came from the shadows a
second before his arms reached for Laura.

"Hey, brother, I would've defended her honor for you."
Butch laughed, and tipped his hat in salute to his elder
sibling.

Laura set her jaw as she looked from one Franklin man
to the other. "I can defend my own honor, thank you,
gentlemen."

"Whoa, you've got yourself a spirited one there!" Max
punched Morgan's arm playfully and touched the brim of
his hat as he turned to Laura. "Pleasure meeting you,
ma'am."

The cowboys ambled toward the bonfire. Their stance
against the orange blaze resembled caricatures of old west
postcards. Two cowboys hats, two sets of bowlegs, silhouetted by the fire. The artist in Laura made her wish she
had brought her camera to the party.

"Would you like coffee?" Morgan guided her toward
the refreshment table.

"Maybe just a soft drink." She wanted to drink in all
the atmosphere of the branding party. The night was an
anachronism for her. The high-tech video editor, so familiar with noisy, pushy Manhattan night life, was absorb-
ing the intimacy, the camaraderie, of the branding party.
Old friends clapped each other's backs and showed off
their children. Neighbors had spent the day helping another
neighbor. The sense of community was strong. These were
people you could count on to be there when you needed
them, Laura realized.

"Would you mind if I introduced you to some more of

my friends?'' Morgan asked courteously. One hand held his coffee cup. The other rested lightly on Laura's hip as his arm stayed protectively across her back.

Countless times throughout the evening, Laura repeated yes, she loved Montana. No, this wasn't a temporary stay, she was here for good. Yes, she was relieved to get out of a high-crime city. No, it wasn't the Ziminski place anymore, it was the Carey place now.

The wolf project drew comments from everyone she met. With very few exceptions, the ranching community was opposed to the program. Still, Laura's point of view was respected. People were willing to accept her for herself, if not for her politics. More than one person teased Morgan about finding such a treasure after all the years of looking.

Moonlight flooded the pasture and a warm breeze from the east kept the temperature from dipping in the thin mountain air. The odor of branded hair had been replaced by the pungency of blue spruce trees edging the pasture, and the spicy cedar wood smoke from the bonfire.

Charlie Barnes's violin led the musicians in jigs and waltzes. As requests were called out from the dancers, another song, and then another, filled the night.

''You're a wonderful dancer, Mr. Franklin,'' Laura complimented her partner.

''Gentler on you than I was on those calves today?'' Morgan teased.

''By far.'' Laura rubbed her cheek against his shoulder and savored the feeling of security he exuded.

His lips rested against her hair as they danced. Her hand lay against the back of his neck, fingers entwined in the hair curling over the collar of his shirt. They moved together, as one body. There was a tinge of regret for both as the music stopped and they separated from each other's arms.

The musicians called for a break and headed to the beer

keg. Some of the younger boys seized the opportunity to bring in a boombox and a stack of CDs. In no time, the pasture filled with the overamplified pounding of country-western rock.

Morgan motioned to a group of cowboys who had helped in the branding.

"I'm going to thank those boys for all their hard work today."

Laura nodded. "You go ahead. I think I'll just sit a minute and soak up this beautiful evening." She watched him walk away from her, relishing every inch of him.

"Can I claim my dance now?"

The young wrangler stood in front of her, his painted-on jeans at eye level with her as she sat. The boy's hat was pushed back on his head now, allowing Laura to see his face. It was young and smooth, free of lines, devoid of character.

"You're on." She extended her hand, which he clasped on his arm and covered with his other hand. He was tall and cute. She could feel youthful energy surging through his body as they walked toward the clearing. Dancers waited for the music to begin. To her surprise, the next song deviated from the frenetic swing rhythm that had been playing. The first twang of the guitar introduction led into a slow, sensuous ballad. The young cowboy's arms closed around Laura.

"You have a name?" She pulled back and stared into his face.

"Brad Worden."

So he was one of the Wordens, Laura thought. Morgan had mentioned their name before, in terms of their huge land holdings in the county. More cattle leaving Montana were Wordens' than from any other producer. He came from money. Enough money, Laura smirked to herself, to buy jeans that fit.

"I'm . . ."

"Laura Carey," he finished for her. "You used to work in a television studio in New York, and you bought the Ziminski place. I asked around."

He held her too tightly for good taste, and she pulled back slightly to send him that message.

"Great party, eh?" She tried to keep the conversation light.

"Why don't you and me take off and go make our own party?"

His family's money and their social standing in the community had evidently taken their toll on his manners, Laura realized.

"I think you'd be more comfortable with somebody closer to your own age." Laura kept the condescension from her voice. "And I'd be more comfortable if you treated me with a little more respect." Her smile softened the sting of her words.

They danced in silence. When the song ended, Brad released her and walked her back to the edge of the crowd.

She held out her hand as Brad turned to leave. "Thanks for the dance, Brad."

"Thank you, ma'am." His hat came off. Shaking her hand, he smiled sheepishly. "You're a nice lady."

The fire was drowned. Lanterns were shut down. Refreshment tables had been folded and stored in the shed. It was dark, with only the moon's light and headlight beams from the ranch truck to illuminate the way. Goodbyes were still echoing down the road to the highway.

"Great party, Mr. Franklin." Laura hugged Morgan tightly. "I had a wonderful day and a terrific night."

"The night's not over." His voice was happy. "I want to follow you home to make sure you make it safely."

"But then it's such a long drive back here for you tonight," she protested.

Even in the darkness, she could see his grin. "You're worth the drive, Laura."

Chapter Eleven

Blue flax and every hue of mountain lupine dotted the landscape as May swept a sunny path into June. Mountain streams pushed aside the last vestiges of winter's snow and rippled freely against their green, grassy banks. Deciduous trees sprouted tender leaves. Cold weather crops—corn, peas, and potatoes—were furrowed into the rich black earth of the Gallatin Valley.

The days lengthened. It was nearly nine each night before the skies became draped in the purple velvet curtains only a mountain twilight produced. It was on one such evening that Laura sat on her pack porch, brushing Tripper and watching Morgan change spark plugs in her lawn mower.

"Do me a favor?" he asked, raising blue eyes to meet hers.

"Sure. What?"

"Marry me."

"Don't joke around, Morgan," Laura dismissed him. "You know how I feel about marriage." Her voice was thick with emotion she tried to hide.

"What are you afraid of? Me?" He grew defensive. Laura had been honest with him about her fear of marriage; he swore to her that they could work it out.

"No." Laura shook her head ferociously. "Me. I just don't think I would be good at marriage. I'm too indepen-

114

dent. So let's just let things alone. What we've got is wonderful the way it is.''

He didn't mention it again that night.

The next day, he didn't call. Summer was on its way and work at the ranch was waiting for him when the sun came up.

The valley prepared for a long, productive summer.

Jason Stillman counted the days until school was out.

Carl Stillman readied his fishing tackle box.

Butch Franklin changed from his black beavertail cowboy hat to a broad-brimmed straw, a sure harbinger of summer.

Laura got warned by the Montana Highway Patrol because she'd neglected to have her studded snow tires removed by May thirty-first.

Tripper teethed and grew. And grew. And grew.

''That dog's going to eat you out of house and home,'' Agnes commented when she and Carl stopped by to deliver starts from their hardy mountain perennials.

''If he doesn't, Morgan will!'' Laura laughed. Morgan was spending more meals at her kitchen table than at the ranch. ''They both have immense appetites. But at least Morgan has better table manners than Tripper.''

She ruffled the dog's fur affectionately and hugged him against her leg. The German shepherd's head rested lovingly on her thigh.

''Wait to put those plants in the ground until after the sun goes down so they don't shock,'' Agnes advised. Newcomers to the area sometimes discounted the intensity of the sun at this altitude.

Carl nudged his wife and laughed. ''After the sun goes down, Morgan probably has better plans for her time.''

''Carl!'' Laura's good-natured response to his ribbing brought color to her cheeks.

Agnes scoffed. ''Now see what you've done, Carl, you've made her blush!''

He gave Laura an affectionate hug. "A woman who can still blush is a woman of quality," he teased.

Agnes nodded in agreement. "Carl's right. You're okay, honey. We're both glad you and Morgan got together."

"Isn't that the truth!" Carl put in. "Old Franklin's smiled more in the past few months than in all the years I've known him."

"Well, I'll try to keep that smile on his face," Laura assured him.

"Marry him. That'll do it." Agnes never beat around the bush.

"It's a big step, Agnes."

"He's got a big heart. It's worth the step."

Tripper sniffed at the bedding plants and pawed at one clumsily, distracting Laura's attention from her friends.

Carl shot his wife a look meant to quell any further mention of marriage. They both knew Laura's stand: her career was very important to her, as was her independence. They could see it in her eyes when anyone broached the subject.

Carl tread on safer ground. "We're going to Rydell's barn raising Saturday. You and Morgan going to be there?"

"You bet," Laura answered, sliding into the vernacular of the area. Before moving to the valley, she'd never heard people respond in the affirmative with those words. Now she caught herself saying it frequently. How easily Montana was molding her! The language, the people, the weather, the life-style. All had become so easy, so completely comfortable to her.

Tripper dropped his ball at Carl's feet and whined.

"One throw, boy, then we've got to get down the road." He overhanded the ball toward the back pasture, sending the dog scurrying to retrieve it. "Penny Wahl's tending the store and she gets real excited if two people pull up to the gas pumps at the same time."

They rattled down the road, leaving one woman, one dog, and a boxful of colorful plants behind.

The house stayed cool during the day, thanks to cross-ventilation from opposing long windows on either side of the house. In the editing room, Laura was lulled into tranquility by the soft breeze wafting through the house, the rhythmic *click-click-click* of the board dials, and the hypnotic blur of videotape whirling through the equipment. Each scene reflecting the wolves' majesty made her yearn to share the beauty with Morgan. The footage wasn't just good, it was great. She had often experienced an abundance of tape with few usable shots. Awkward camera angles and incomplete shots could turn otherwise good footage into waste because scenes could not be cut and edited to best advantage. Paul's work was top-notch. It was a pleasure to work the scenes and arrange frames into a smooth-flowing work of art.

Morgan came for dinner and taught Tripper how to sit up. When they left, the woman and her dog watched his truck pull away and thought how much they enjoyed having him around.

Moonbeams angled through the lacy curtains of Laura's bedroom and bathed the room in blue light as Laura lay studying the tape log for tomorrow's work. She could hardly contain her excitement for the wolf project. It was the culmination of all her professional dreams.

In the morning, Laura poured a cup of tea and thought of Morgan. She realized how accustomed she had become to thinking of him first thing in the morning. And all day. And at night, when she looked at the moon.

Her days were fully scheduled with work. Faxes, calls, letters, e-mail, packages of tape coming in and completed log sheets filled her waking hours, punctuated with brief breaks when she and Tripper played or gardened or walked.

Her evenings were filled with Morgan. They cooked

supper together, and washed dishes afterward. She marveled at his huge, tanned hands plunging deep into dishwater and doing domestic chores without a fuss.

He entertained her with shadow animals he made by moving his hands in the light.

She held him fascinated by shaping a paper towel into a dove.

He explored a scar on her knee, the result from a bicycle wreck when she was ten.

She listened and held him tenderly when he remembered the way his grandmother's hands formed pie dough.

One evening after dishes were stacked neatly in the cupboard, Laura turned to find him squirting a message with mustard on the kitchen counter.

Marry me, Laura, it read.

She laughed and rubbed it out with a sponge. ''Marriage would spoil our beautiful arrangement, and that mustard will stain the counter.''

On Saturday morning, the jangling phone awoke her earlier than she wanted to be awakened.

''Good morning, glory,'' he sang to her softly. She laughed. He was no Hal Ketchum. His voice was mellow and low, but Nashville wouldn't beat a path to his door.

''Good morning to you!'' she crooned softly. ''We've got a barn to build today.''

''I'll be there in half an hour. Wear your barn-building britches.''

She was still laughing when she heard his truck pull into the drive twenty minutes later.

It's a gaggle of geese and a covey of quail, Laura thought. What did they call a group of pickup trucks gathered for a barn raising? A flock of Fords? A den of Dodges? The vehicles were parallel along the fence line leading into Elmer Rydell's farmyard. Just as first-time visitors to Manhattan were amazed by the abundance of yellow taxicabs, Laura found the profusion of pickups fascinating. Each vehicle held the requisite gun rack, and more than one sported a bumper sticker reading, *Keep Montana Green: Shoot a Land Developer.*'' Strong people with strong convictions, these residents of the area. Laura smiled to herself.

Rydell's place had been woven into the tapestry of the canyon nearly a century earlier. Homesteaded by Elmer's grandparents, the ranch continued to raise registered Angus cattle.

Several months before, Elmer's wife Grace had put a batch of garbage in the burn barrel down the path from the barn. It had been a windy day, and the protective screen lid blew off the burn barrel while Elmer and Grace were on the other side of the mountain feeding livestock. Sparks had blown into the dry shake roof of their aging barn and had ignited the building in just minutes. They were left with a gutted, charred heap of timbers and little else after flames engulfed the building. Now, their neighbors had gathered to raise a new barn on the spot.

Unhooking hammers from tool belts, the workers began turning the stacks of lumber into skeletal walls. The staccato hammering continued all morning. Pitchers of lemonade and coffee were drained. The pounding continued. Buzzing circular saws screeched above the noise of pummeling hammers. Punctuating the scene were shouts of the men as they created section after section of the new building. The sides and trusses waited while ropes were attached to bring the large sections of the frame into place. It was hard work, made easy by the number of helping hands.

At noon, tools were set aside and workers scurried down ladders and off scaffolding to the repast awaiting them in the farmyard. As it was with branding, Laura could see that the work accomplished was almost a secondary function of the gathering. It was the social interaction they sought. It was a helping of hands, a roll call of support.

Laura looked at the progress of the building with awe. A hundred years ago, had a group of Montana pioneers gathered to erect the barn that had burned? Did those people sit in the sunshine and share their food and talents and dreams? Was one of the carpenters loved by a woman as much as she loved Morgan? And what had happened to that love when the barn was built and the day was done? Did they marry and have children who were now old, old people themselves?

"You're thinkin' awful hard there, girl." Morgan's arms clasped her around the waist and he nuzzled her neck as she stood near the serving table in the farmyard.

"Daydreaming. Wondering about the day the original barn was built."

"Probably saw a crowd much like today's. Except there'd be wagons over there"—he nodded toward the trucks—"and you wouldn't be wearing those venom denims." He rolled his eyes and grinned, noting his appreciation of her tight jeans.

"I'd have a sunbonnet and long sleeves to keep my skin milky white and soft, just like a lady should be," she joked.

"And you'd have a wedding ring on your finger before you broke the barn carpenter's heart," Morgan added. His voice had lost its lightness.

"Don't, Morgan." She walked toward the table and filled a plate.

"So tell me how you like Montana." Grace Rydell's eyes were like sapphires in her weathered face. She patted to a spot beside her on the picnic bench, and Laura sat down beside her.

"I like it very much. I'm very happy here."

"Well, we're happy to have you." Her jack-o'-lantern

grin was infectious and Laura found herself warming instantly to this woman.

Morgan straddled the picnic bench and sat down next to Laura.

"And I'll bet this guy's pretty happy to have you around, too!" Grace squeezed Morgan's hand. "You're a special one," she told him. "Your mama would be so proud of you boys."

The meal was over too quickly and the crew went back to work, pounding and sawing and planing and measuring.

It was dark when the trucks snaked caravan-fashion down the road to the highway, and scattered in separate directions to return to their respective homes.

Silence, oppressive and shroudlike, hung in the truck as Morgan drove down the canyon. Laura chalked it up to a full day's work: the sun and the barn building had drained everyone's energy.

They bumped across the road from the turnoff and drove in silence to Laura's house.

Pulling up in front of the gate, Morgan left the engine idling on the truck as he got out, circled in front of the hood, and opened the door for his passenger. He released the tailgate of the truck and whistled for Tripper to jump down.

"Thanks for coming today," he said quietly. His eyes avoided hers.

She stood outside the gate, her dog at her side. Morgan turned and started back toward the truck.

"Come in for a cup of coffee? Tea? Apple juice?" Laura tried to squelch the quiver in her voice. Something was very, very wrong here.

"I don't think so."

"Morgan, are you mad at me? What did I do?"

"Nothing."

"Something's wrong." She followed him to the truck and pulled his arm toward her. "Tell me."

"Let's go inside, Laura. I don't want to discuss this in the middle of the road."

Tripper bounced to the door, followed by his mistress and by the man she loved.

"I'll get coffee," Laura called over her shoulder as the door slammed. "Sit down and relax."

Coffee and dog biscuits came out of the cupboard. Laura balanced two cups of coffee in one hand and flicked on the parlor light switch with the other.

"Here."

"Thanks."

"Sure."

Is my world going to end with monosyllabic words? Laura wondered. What in the heck was happening?

"Talk," she instructed.

"I don't know if I can go on seeing you, Laura." Morgan shook his head. She saw the frustration in his face, heard it in his voice.

"Why? What in the world has happened since we left here this morning, all cheerful and excited about the barn building? We're the same people as we were this morning. What has you so upset?"

"Everybody at Rydell's today knows me." Morgan set his jaw resolutely and continued. "They've known me since I was just a kid. They knew my folks and respected them. And I grew up and earned their respect." He sipped slowly on the hot coffee.

"And?"

"And they know I'm a man of honor. I've always tried to deal fairly with people when I do business. My word is my bond." Again, his coffee cup tipped up.

"How does this—"

"I realized today," he interrupted Laura, setting his cup on the table and getting up to pace the floor, "I realized how deeply ingrained my feelings are about things like honor and respect. Part of love is honor, Laura. I want to be proud of our love. I don't want to pick you up for a date and drop you off and go home like we're nothing to each other. Do you understand what I mean? I want something substantial that I can count on. Commitment for a lifetime, Laura. I want to marry you. I don't want to play games.''

''And you feel obligated to marry me because the neighbors know we've been dating steadily the last few months?'' Laura was outraged.

''No. My only obligation is to have you accorded the respect you're due. The whole valley knows the way we feel about each other. Around here, when two people have those feelings, they make a commitment to each other.''

''And if the commitment doesn't last?'' Laura asked sarcastically. It was killing her inside to hear Morgan forcing the issue. She had been satisfied with the status quo. Why wasn't he?

''Then it isn't a commitment, is it? It's an empty promise. A real commitment is a lifetime thing, whether you promise to feed and love a dog until it dies, or you make the same promise to a man. If you don't have any more faith than that in yourself, Laura, how are you going to have any in me?''

''Morgan, it's not a question of faith in you. I've already told you it's me, it's not you. I just don't know if I believe in marriage. My parents had a rotten marriage, and I'll never forget it.''

''You were a young girl, not an adult. Now you're a woman. You're capable of making a mature decision now.''

''I'll tell you what I'm capable of, Morgan, and that's realizing what a bad decision can do to your life. It's watching my mother spend her life complaining because she had no identity outside of being a wife and mother. She felt smothered by marriage and she never quit blaming my father for robbing her independence. She made his life miserable along with hers.''

''As long as you love me, Laura, you couldn't make me miserable.''

''I won't give up my work and my identity. And I sure as the dickens won't give up this place I'm working so hard for. I love you, Morgan, but I have to be Laura Carey. I can't be Mrs. Franklin.''

Morgan wiped his brow. ''Then keep your name. Stay Laura Carey. Or hyphenate it. Keep your job. And keep this place.'' His voice was low and controlled. ''You don't have to give up anything to be my wife.''

She shook her head, her hair catching the light as it settled back onto her shoulders. ''I set goals for myself when I moved here. I would pay for this place. It would be my own corner of the world. I'd build a successful business. It's important to me.''

''More important to you than I am?''

''You're talking apples and oranges, Morgan. I didn't want to fall in love. I didn't plan it. It just happened, okay? But I will not put aside the goals I set for myself. Not for you, not for anybody.''

Morgan stopped pacing. ''Sounds like your mind is made up.'' He reached down and ruffled Tripper's fur.

''See ya, Trip.'' He patted the dog's head and looked up at Laura. ''Good-bye, Laura.''

''You can't be serious! You'd walk out that door over whether or not we get married? Why can't we just go on the way we have been?'' She heard her voice rising, and despite hating the shrillness of it, she continued. ''I'm not the first woman you've kissed and I know darned well if you go out that door, I won't be the last. So you decide if it's worth throwing away what we mean to each other.''

''What we mean to each other isn't worth a hill of beans if five months or five years from now it's not going to be here. If I can't count on you being part of my whole life, Laura, I'm going to have to get out of yours.''

In stiff, quick strides, he was across the room and out the door. Laura heard the truck door slam as he pulled away and started down the road.

Tripper jumped on the couch and parted the curtains with his nose to peer out the window. He barked as the truck taillights disappeared into the night.

What amazed Laura the most was knowing that despite the fact Morgan had taken her heart with him, she could still feel it breaking.

Chapter Twelve

Kelly Hancock hooked her wardrobe bag over the closet door in Laura's spare bedroom and unzipped it. She pulled out a pair of jeans and threw them on the bed.

Tripper, who had become her devoted companion during the ride from the airport, beat a tattoo with his tail and looked adoringly at the redhead.

"Well, Tripper, after I get these jeans on, we're going to take your mother for a walk."

Leaping from the foot of the bed in a single bound, the dog ran expectantly to the back door.

"He knows 'walk.' " Laura smiled from the doorway. " 'Eat' and 'walk' are his two favorite words."

Kelly's eye were drawn to her friend. The shock of Laura's appearance when she arrived at the airport had subsided. It was more than the weight loss. It was the total lack of spirit in Laura's eyes that unnerved Kelly. The person before her was like an empty shell of the Laura Carey whom Kelly adored.

There was more, Kelly realized. There was the wounded, hurt look that drained Laura's face when her friend mentioned Morgan Franklin.

"We'll talk about that when we get to the house," Laura had answered.

"Ready?" Laura opened the back door and let Tripper go out ahead of her. Kelly folded her thick, springy red curls under a baseball cap and followed the two down the back steps and out into the pasture.

Laura pointed out the mountain flora as they walked: salvia, columbine, wild strawberries, shepherd's oak.

''I've been here six hours''—Kelly consulted her watch—''and you haven't mentioned what happened between you and him.''

''Him?''

''Him. The 'him' who's filled your heart and our conversations and faxes for the past three months. Now you can't even say his name. What's up?''

Laura visibly whitened but kept the pace hiking on the trail toward the river. Her eyes misted with unshed tears. Kelly knew she'd struck a nerve.

''Nothing,'' Laura said at length. ''It's over, that's all.''

''That's all? Laura, from the time you first faxed me about him, he's all you've talked about. Morgan this, Morgan that. He gave you Tripper, he gave you his love, and now you're saying it's over? You're not your same old self, girl. You're miserable. I never thought I'd see you so hung up like this on any guy, but it's happened. I can tell in your voice when you talk about him. Have you two tried to resolve the problem?''

''It's done, Kelly.'' Laura's voice was barely audible above the coursing river water as they plopped down on the sunny bank.

''Does he want it to be over?''

''You don't see him around, do you?'' Cynicism crept into Laura's voice. ''He walked out the door almost a month ago and he hasn't been back. He hasn't called. He hasn't stopped to see Tripper. It's over.''

The sun grew hot on the two women as they lounged on the river bank, throwing sticks at the water's edge for the dog to retrieve.

''It's a relief, really.'' Laura sighed. ''When you quit

seeing Raleigh Newhall, didn't you like having more time to yourself?''

Kelly smiled at the thought of the egotistical, self-absorbed man with whom she had recently broken off dating.

''No.'' Her answer was blunt. ''I liked having a guy around. But we were too different, and besides, it was purely superficial. I didn't fall in love. You did.''

''Whatever love means. I didn't think loving somebody could hurt this badly.'' Laura watched Tripper dislodge a stone from underwater. ''Oh well, heck. No man's loyalty will ever match a dog's.'' She tried to laugh, but her voice broke.

''So you're miserable without Morgan. He must really be something. What's the future in that?''

''There is none. But I'm fine.''

''Sure.'' Kelly nodded in agreement. ''You're just fine. You've lost—what?—twenty pounds you could ill afford to lose. Your eyes look like a zombie's. You've lost your enthusiasm for everything. You haven't even talked about your wolf documentary, which is all you could talk about before that cowboy walked into your life. You haven't even asked about the gang at the TV studio, because your whole world is tied to some devil in denim who's broken your heart.''

The sculptor in Kelly won out as she scooped a handful of mud, thick with bentonite, from the river's edge and slapped it between her palms. ''You fell in love for the first time in your life, Laura Carey.'' She pointed one muddied finger at her friend, scolding her lovingly. ''I don't know what went wrong, but something sure did. And it sounds like you're too stubborn to talk it out with him.''

Laura's folded arms shielded her eyes from the sun as she lay on her back, soaking in the warmth of the summer afternoon sun. It was easier to talk that way, and the whole story tumbled out.

"Now," Laura concluded, "there's nothing more to it. Nothing's ever going to change. I never should've come here."

"Now wait a minute. You knew exactly what you were getting into when you moved here. You had your Montana dream and nothing would stop you."

"I still do. I'll never give up my place."

"Nobody says you have to." Kelly punched the ball of clay and started molding it with her fingers. "Heck, I have both an apartment and a separate art studio. If you married Morgan, you could still keep your place for work."

"It's too late to think about it."

"It's never too late if you really love him." Kelly pinched and twisted the clay in her hands.

"Hey, pal." Laura sat upright and, with false bravado, changed the subject. She tossed a pebble toward her sculpting friend. "Paul Caro called last week. The Burlington nomination committee requested a copy of our wolf documentary." *There,* she thought to herself, *I'm already back to my old self again, talking about films.*

"Does that pretty much assure a nomination?"

"Heavens, no. They review hundreds of projects. But at least they're aware of it."

"You can do it, girl."

"Picture this." Laura held up her hands as if framing in a scene. "A Burlington Award on my mantel, right next to the dog sculpture you made me."

It sounded hollow to Laura, even as she said it. The only thing she could picture in her parlor that would bring her joy right now, would be a certain tall, skinny cowboy.

Kelly cupped her hands around the bust of Tripper she had fashioned from the clump of bentonite, and lay it beside Laura on the rocky beach.

The music at O'Grady's Inn poured out into the parking lot as Laura, Agnes, Becky Trask, and Kelly walked from the car. The steady, pounding bass guitar signaled live music tonight.

Agnes put her arm around Kelly's shoulder and teased the redhead. "Tonight, we're going to find you a good-lookin' cowboy to take back to New York."

"If God wanted me to love a cowboy, I would've been born Dale Evans," Kelly retorted. "I came here to comfort my buddy, not fall in love."

The two older women looked at each other and then at Laura. They too had noticed, as Kelly had, the weight loss and sad look burdening their friend these days.

Agnes Stillman had seen Morgan when he came in the store the week before. Never had she seen a man more tortured, she told Becky Trask afterward on the phone. He was quiet and sullen, a different man from the happy charmer who couldn't keep away from Laura at the branding party dance.

"It's none of our business, whatever the trouble is," Carl had warned Agnes.

"If Laura cut her hand, I'd bandage it. It's her heart that's hurt, and I'm going to do whatever I can to help." Agnes had been adamant. They belonged together, that girl and Morgan Franklin, and if she could help them get back together, she would.

"The dancing girls have arrived!" Clara Chandler's voice boomed out over the music. Every head turned toward the door as the four women entered. "How're you tonight, ladies?"

"Hi, Clara!" Three voices answered in unison. Kelly, never shy, introduced herself to the flamboyant waitress and eyed a cowboy across the room.

"Don't tell me you ladies are unchaperoned?" Clara asked in mock horror.

"Girls' night out." Laura grinned. "Kelly's been asking about our Wild West nightlife, and we figured this is where we'd find it!"

"Set yourself down, gals, and I'll bring you some spiced cider." Clara's order book was all between her ears, and she sashayed off to fill the drinks while the women found a table.

"Real atmosphere," Kelly commented dryly, eying the stuffed moose head over the bar and the rodeo pictures lining the walls. In the corner, a cowboy with a huge beer belly and bright red suspenders threw his hip against a pinball machine.

"Real west," Agnes added.

"Real loud," Becky put in.

"I think you've got an admirer, Kelly." Laura laughed as she noticed Wayne Roscoe sauntering across the dance floor with his eyes glued on the bouncy redhead.

"Hi, ladies," he said smoothly, and tipped his cowboy hat.

"Wayne Roscoe, Kelly Hancock." Laura offered the introduction.

"New in town?" The cowboy tilted his head to show off his strong jaw. He considered conceit a flaw, and knew he had no flaws.

"Just visiting." Kelly's explanation was brief. In her mind, she had died and gone to Hades. Did Laura actually like this music? She looked at the crowd around the bar. Were they all trying out for parts in a Hopalong Cassidy movie?

Four steaming ciders graced Clara's tray as she swooped through the crowd and handed the drinks around.

"Drink up! You're in the west now, girl." Becky laughed. "Once, after a rodeo, I saw a man ride his horse right through that door and up to the bar."

The stories flew. Comparisons of Kelly's New York lifestyle and Laura's metamorphosis into a Montana woman brought gales of laughter from the group. Kelly's rapier wit kept the mood high. For the first time in the weeks since she last saw Morgan, Laura was laughing.

"You girls are having way too much fun."

Laura felt a hand rest on each of her shoulders. She turned, stiffly, the laughter leaving her eyes.

"Hi, Butch."

She felt his hands tighten momentarily, as if to reassure her.

"Hi, Laura, ladies. Wayne," Butch acknowledged the man at Kelly's side.

Butch leaned across the table, his hand reaching toward Kelly. "Butch Franklin," he introduced himself.

"Kelly Hancock." Her grip, muscled from years of sculpting, was firm as she clasped Butch's hand in hers.

Butch was surprised at the strength of the woman's shake.

"Laura's friend from New York?" Butch remembered hearing about Kelly: her red hair, her talent, her loyalty to Laura.

"Yes. Morgan Franklin's brother?" Kelly returned. She felt as though she knew him already: his sense of humor, his enthusiasm, his friendship with Laura.

Butch nodded, then motioned toward a vacant chair at the next table. "May I join you folks?"

Remembering her manners, Laura pulled the chair into the circle surrounding their table and smiled at Butch. "Please do."

The music throbbed in their throats. Bass guitars thumped, the keyboard shrieked, and dancers twirled back and forth on the dance floor.

As Wayne and Kelly left the table to dance, Agnes and Becky decided to visit the ladies' room. Laura was left alone with Butch.

"How've you been?" His concern was as much for her as for his brother.

"Work's going well. Everything's great. Just great."

"Liar."

Laura clenched her hands together to hide their trembling. Her pride wouldn't allow her to drop her guard, even with Butch.

"Look." She sighed. "I'm sure you know Morgan and I are no longer seeing each other."

"I know he's thrown himself into work on the ranch until he's wearing himself out. He's fixed every section of fence that's ever started leaning, and cleaned sheds and stables until they shine. He never quits from daylight until after dark. And he doesn't talk to anybody. He's miserable."

Good, Laura thought. *Let him be miserable. Let him feel just a fraction of the pain I feel every minute of the day.*

"He's a big boy. He'll live."

"But it's you he wants to live with."

Laura picked at the corner of her paper coaster. "Only if he can live under his rules." She levelled her eyes at the cowboy and searched for understanding in his face. "Well, there's no use talking about it. It's over."

"For good?"

Laura's laugh was hollow. "For good? Heavens no, Butch. There's nothing good about it. Do you think I want to go through each day feeling like I swallowed a brick?" Her guard was down; she couldn't stop her anger from pouring out. "I never should've gotten into this."

From the dance floor, Kelly saw the anguish on her friend's face. Why did Butch Franklin have to show up and wreck everybody's good time? Agnes and Becky were deep in conversation across the room. They weren't noticing Laura's misery.

"Let's sit this one out." Kelly grabbed Wayne Roscoe by the arm and pulled him outside the crowd of dancers. She returned to the table, in time to hear Laura's remark. One Franklin had already hurt Laura; her friend wasn't going to let Butch add to her heartache.

"Teach me to dance to this music?" she invited Butch.

His look of surprise matched Laura's. Gamely, he rose and led the assertive redhead to the dance floor.

A waltz brought couples closely together as arms entwined, bodies swayed slowly, and guitars pulsated.

"So how do you fit into this whole picture with Laura and your brother?" Kelly's directness startled him. *This is one up-front woman,* he thought admiringly.

"I'm Laura's friend. I'm Morgan's friend, too."

A frown creased Kelly's brow. "Laura's my best friend. And I don't want anybody hurting her."

Butch's arm tightened around his dance partner. "Morgan's my best friend. And I don't like seeing him hurt either. Right now he's hurting pretty badly."

"So you're blaming Laura, are you?"

You don't have that red hair for nothing, Butch mused.

"No." His answer was slow, deliberate. "No more than I blame Morgan. They're two fiercely independent people who just happened to fall in love with each other. But Morgan's got some pretty set ideas. One of them is that people in love get married."

"So he can keep her barefoot and pregnant? Welcome to the twentieth century, Cowboy!"

"Whoa!" Butch stopped in the middle of the dancers and stared down at his adversary. "What have you got against marriage?"

"Nothing."

"Have you ever tried it?"

Kelly shook her head, her green eyes flashing. "No."

"Well, I have," Butch admitted. "It didn't work out. But it didn't sour me to the point where I wouldn't try it again someday."

"Laura's not soured on marriage. She's just scared."

Frustration knotted Butch's shoulders. "And you think Morgan's not scared? Heck, he's been single his whole life, and now this gorgeous, long-legged creature comes along and turns his world upside down. And when he tries to do right by her and marry her, she throws it in his face.''

''Do right by her?'' Kelly dropped her hand from Butch's shoulder and ceased dancing. ''Can you hear how archaic you sound? For heaven's sake, she isn't wearing a scarlet letter on her bodice. You seem to think he's obligated to marry her!''

Clenching his teeth in anger, Butch set his jaw. Across the room, Laura and her female companions were listening to Wayne Roscoe. Knowing Wayne, Butch realized, he would be talking about himself.

''Is that what you think?'' Kelly repeated. ''You think he feels obligated to marry her?''

''I'm saying . . .'' he spoke slowly, distinctly, to the red-headed dynamo facing him, ''. . . Morgan wants Laura to be his wife. Forever. If she doesn't want to be, then he's done the only thing he can do. He's gotten out of her life. Which is probably the smartest thing a cowboy can do when some fancy city woman catches his eye.''

He turned on his heel and left his partner standing alone on the dance floor.

''Last call for alcohol!'' The bandleader made his announcement over the microphone, and a wave of cowboys stampeded to the bar to fill their final drink orders of the evening.

''May I see you home, ma'am?'' Wayne Roscoe asked Kelly in his finest aw-shucks cowboy affectation.

''I came with Laura, but thanks.'' Kelly's eyes scoured the bar for Butch. She hadn't meant to make him mad. But in spite of herself, she knew she had succeeded in doing just that.

The night air was heavy with the smell of evergreens and sagebrush as the women loaded into the car and drove down the canyon.

''What a gorgeous night,'' Becky commented, rolling

down the window. A night out with her friends was a relaxing change of pace from the farming which had begun in earnest at the Trask place.

Agnes agreed. "Just nice to get out." And nice to get home again to Carl and Jason, she thought to herself. She had seen the emptiness in Laura's eyes tonight when Butch had failed to return to their table. Any reminder of Morgan, even his brother, made Laura sad, Agnes realized.

They dropped Becky at her place and continued down the highway to the store, where a light in the living quarters welcomed Agnes home. The road was nearly deserted as Laura drove through the darkness.

"Is it always this dark?" Kelly asked, incredulous.

"Darker, on a first-quarter moon. Lighter in the winter with the reflection off the snow."

"You've turned into a regular country bumpkin, Laura Carey," Kelly teased. "You wouldn't even be comfortable in Manhattan anymore."

"Oh, I'd be comfortable visiting there, but I wouldn't stay away from here very long. This is home for me."

Headlights bounced off sagebrush and pines bordering the road. Laura hit her high beams, illuminating the dark lane more clearly as she peered through the windshield.

Eyes, luminescent green, caught in the reflection of her headlights and moved swiftly from the roadside. Instinctively, Laura braked.

"What's wrong?" Kelly's hand braced against the dashboard.

"There's an animal near the road. I just saw its eyes."

Kelly scrutinized the darkness. "What was it?"

Laura shrugged and continued cautiously down the road. "It looked too big for a coyote. Maybe somebody's big dog is out on the loose."

"As long as it's not Bigfoot." Kelly laughed. "I don't want to be next week's tabloid headline when I've been abducted as Bigfoot's love slave."

''Speaking of love slave, what did you think of Wayne Roscoe?''

''Big belt buckle, bigger hat, biggest ego.''

Laura laughed softly. ''He told me when I met him,'' she confided, ''that he didn't like tall women, so I shouldn't expect a date with him.''

''Are you serious?''

''Completely. He was at Jim and Becky Trask's party and he spent most of the night watching his own reflection in the front room window!'' *And I spent most of my time,* Laura recalled, *watching Morgan dance with Janelle Harding.*

''What about Butch Franklin?'' Kelly's voice stirred her from her thoughts.

''What about him?'' Laura made a vain attempt to dislodge Morgan's image from her mind and concentrate on Kelly's question.

''He's sexy,'' Kelly insisted.

''He is?''

''You haven't noticed?'' The redhead was incredulous.

''He's really fun. He's got a great personality.''

Kelly scoffed. ''You make him sound like a cocker spaniel.''

Reaching the farmstead, they parked and started up the path to the house. A myriad of stars peppered the raven sky. The yard light danced across Kelly's copper hair as Laura followed her friend. The moon remained a silent sentinel over the valley. Following the creek where it snaked through Laura's north pasture, a lone gray wolf crept silently in the silver lunar light.

Chapter Thirteen

With the same intensity that drove winter cold through flesh and straight to the bone, Montana delivered summer in an insistent, scorching barrage of sweltering days and warm, still nights. Sun glared on the grain fields, drying them to pale amber. Bees drawn to the flowering hedge at the far corner of the Carey place buzzed lazily in the sweltering afternoon heat. Tripper lay under a shading cottonwood tree near the creek, his tongue hanging to the side as he panted heartily. Across the field, the report of fireworks echoed through the valley. The dog's ears perked at the sound, then relaxed as he realized there was no imminent danger.

"Too hot to cook," Kelly huffed, cocooned in the back porch hammock. "Let's order Chinese food."

Laura added another folded towel to the stack of laundry and grinned. "Kelly, after being here three weeks, you still forget we're not the in the middle of Manhattan. There's no Chinese restaurant within fifty miles. We can run into town and eat, or we can settle for some fresh fruit and bagels."

"Something light. Butch is taking me out to dinner tonight."

"I'm glad you've become friends. When he left here last night, I thought he was going to have to be surgically removed from your side."

An infusion of color in Kelly's face let Laura know she'd hit her mark.

"He's just a great guy," the redhead offered. "You don't mind my going out with him?"

"Why would I?"

"Because he's Morgan's brother."

"Butch is my friend, Kelly. He can't help what happened between Morgan and me. I want you to enjoy Butch. He's wonderful. I adore him." She balanced the laundry basket on her hip as she opened the screen door. It slammed behind her. In a minute, she was back outdoors. She slouched into the rocking chair and crossed her long, tanned legs at the ankles, resting on the porch railing.

The shade provided a respite from the glaring sun. A bouquet of wildflowers Kelly had picked sat drooping in their pottery crock on the steps. Tripper ambled up the path from the field and panted enthusiastically at the sight of Laura.

"Trip, darlin', come out of the sun. You're too hot."

Tripper had passed his three-month birthday last week. Long-legged and still clumsy, the dog only grew more precious to Laura each day. How she had ever lived without him, she couldn't comprehend.

"Tripper's growing," she pointed out to her friend.

Kelly dropped her arm from the mesh of the hammock and pursed her lips to whistle at the dog. "Here, Trip. Let me see how big you're getting."

Crossing the porch in one ungainly bound, he landed on Kelly's lap. Her face was sloshed with affectionate wet licks as he wagged from his tail to his shoulders.

"Morgan hasn't even called to see how he is," Laura agonized. "I thought he cared about him."

"He cares about both of you, Laura. But he has his pride."

"Archaic pride."

"You could call him."

Kelly's suggestion went unheeded.

"Come with us," Kelly pleaded that afternoon, "or I won't go either." The fourth of July celebration included a barbecue and fireworks show at Rainbow Lake.

"Go enjoy the program," Laura insisted. "I've got so much work to do, and besides, you and Butch don't need a chaperon."

"Then I'll stay home and keep you company while you work."

"Kelly, go!"

"Come with us."

"I'd better stay home." It was a familiar response to invitations. Laura knew the chance of running into Morgan grew with each social activity in the community. She couldn't see him, couldn't risk feeling her heart break any further.

"We'll stay too, then." Kelly was resolute. Nothing would sway her, once her mind was made up.

When Butch arrived, Kelly informed him of her decision. He agreed. They all went, or they all stayed.

"All for one," Butch chanted, "and one for all."

"We're not the Three Musketeers." Laura chuckled. "We're not joined at the hip. Besides, I can't leave Tripper. The fireworks might scare him."

"Let him stay inside."

"And you'll rebuild any table legs he chews?" Laura challenged Butch.

"He's outgrown that chewing business, haven't you, Tripper?" Butch ruffled the dog's ears affectionately.

"As long as he has teeth," Laura said with a laugh, "he'll be a chewer."

"Come with us," Kelly asked again.

Butch chimed in, "We insist."

"Tripper, will you be okay out back until I get home?" Laura questioned him, rubbing her chin softly against his forehead. "The fireworks won't hurt you."

The dog wiggled his tail enthusiastically and followed them until they got into Butch's truck.

"Tripper, stay," Laura ordered the dog firmly. She checked the side mirror as Butch pulled away from the house. The German shepherd was walking back toward the house, his tail drooped in dejection.

Tricolored bunting draped from post to post on the picnic pavilion at Rainbow Lake. Barbecue tables lined the wooded area beside the building, topped with red checkered tablecloths. Two immense outdoor grills sizzled with hamburgers and hot dogs. Red, white, and blue balloons danced leisurely in the scant breeze.

Shirley Nygaard sat fanning herself with the edge of her straw hat.

"Hot enough for you?"

Laura, Kelly, and Butch set their picnic coolers on the bench next to her.

"Plenty hot," Butch agreed.

Where had everyone come from? Laura wondered. There were people inside the cabin, more on the shaded porch, and a crowd in the woods. She didn't know this many people lived in the valley. Sun-browned ranchers in straw hats and short-sleeved shirts were deep in conversation. Ranch wives swapped recipes and gardening tips. Children of every size, with wet T-shirts and shorts plastered to them, frolicked at the lake's edge.

How many pounds of hamburger were served that day, no one could guess. Mounds of salad disappeared as quickly as it was put out. The afternoon's picnic was, undoubtedly, a smashing success.

A tug-of-war, a three-legged race, and an egg toss held the attention of both participants and audience alike. The clink of ringers from the horseshoe-throwing contest rang across the beach. Two groups of barbershop singers roamed through the crowds, harmonizing and encouraging people to sing along.

"I feel like I'm in a fifties movie." Kelly grinned. "I didn't think celebrations like this really existed anymore."

"Simple pleasures are simple treasures," Laura quoted philosophically.

Nowhere in the county did the sun set as flamboyantly as at Rainbow Lake. As the afternoon slipped unobtrusively into twilight, the bright whiteness that had glared relentlessly all day blossomed into a vibrant orange and slipped gently from the sky. As it settled on the horizon, its ghostly reflection shimmered golden on the water's surface. The sky, startlingly blue, held the ball of fire a moment longer, suspended, before allowing it to slip beyond its grasp.

The sound of the tide lapping at the lake's edge was hypnotic. Laura stood watching a raft full of youngsters heading back to shore. Their laughter skipped across the water, the gay exuberance of carefree youth. Splashing and shouting, living and laughing—it was the sound of summer. Montanans joked that their year consisted of nine months of winter and three months of company. The lure of summer sunshine and warm evenings on the water had brought people out in force.

Kicking off her strap sandals, Laura waded into the cool water. She ventured out until the gentle waves sloshed against her knees. In the descending darkness the lake held a certain magic.

A skyrocket burst above the crowd, signaling the start of the fireworks show. Its spidery shower of sparks plummeted earthward and met its reflection in the water. Following it, a flurry of Roman candles displayed a plethora of fire-hued fountains.

The acrid smell of gunpowder filled the air as children lit string after string of firecrackers. The hollow *pop-pop-pop* resonated on the beach. As one aerial display after another erupted in the sky, the audience's collective oohs and ahhs registered their approval. The moon, bright and full, competed with multicolor starbursts against the black, cloudless sky.

Children weaved in and out of the crowd. A special magic came with summer in this part of the country that had so little warm weather. The energy level was frenetic, as though youngsters had to make up for all the months of winter they had been stuck indoors. Farming equipment had been stilled for the day. Haying was postponed temporarily, this was the time to celebrate. Bonfires along the beach licked the darkness. The camaraderie of old friends resounded in laughter and conversations dotting the night. Bits and pieces of dialogue floated in and out of hearing as Laura walked along the beach: remember the time when we . . . you never saw such a hailstorm . . . should have put on sunscreen . . . depends on the price per bushel . . . sent in the 2nd Battalion, Third Marines . . . then I says to him . . .

Couples strolled along the shoreline, arm in arm, silhouetted against the luminescent moonglow on the water. The freedom of being outdoors, the gaiety of the occasion, suffused the night with an aura of expectation. How could anyone not be happy on a night like this? It was made for lovers. Kelly and Butch were farther down the beach, their heads tipped toward each other in rapt attention. Whatever Butch was saying, it was obvious Kelly was hanging on to his every word.

The memory of her times with Morgan tormented Laura. *That's how* we *were,* she thought. *Wanting to know everything about each other.* Their discovery of each other's worlds led them on a fascinating journey. Laura thirsted for stories Morgan told about his Montana childhood. He in turn quizzed her about her family, her Peace Corps years, her career. Every joke was funnier when Morgan told it; every newspaper story became more interesting when he read it aloud to her. Each day was sunnier when she saw his smile. Sunsets were more poignant when viewed from the circle of his arms.

She remembered the excitement of picking up the phone to hear his low, soft greeting when he called in the middle of the night just to say he loved her.

It took her breath away, this feeling of loss.

Pausing at a dry spot on the beach, Laura bent to re-buckle the thin straps of her sandals. The welcome, cool evening air after the scorching day refreshed her. Pulling the heavy braid off her back, she held it against her head and let the hint of breeze caress her neck.

"Hello, Laura." Janelle Harding's smile held a smugness Laura found nearly intolerable.

"Janelle." She recovered quickly. "How are you?"

The diminutive blonde posed in her stylish linen suit, aware of the contrast between it and Laura's cutoff blue jeans and casual top. She ran a manicured hand through her artfully highlighted hair and closed her eyes dramatically. "I'm exhausted. Working on this Fourth of July celebration has taken all my time," she griped. A realtor by trade, Janelle used community activities as a means of meeting prospective clients and, according to Butch, eligible men.

"You should be proud of your efforts, Janelle. The crowds here tonight certainly attest to the success of the project." Laura looked at the groups of people still enjoying the festivities.

"I hope people do appreciate the time it takes to put something like this on," Janelle continued to grumble, as much to herself as to Laura. Brightening, she rolled her eyes in an affectation of innocence and smiled. "Why, Morgan and I were up before daybreak today to get everything ready for tonight. Well"—she never lost a beat—"take care, won't you, Laura?"

She turned and ankled up the beach, her hips twitching

as she minced her steps. Laura watched until the darkness enveloped the woman.

She had to let me know, Laura fumed. *She just had to mention his name and let me know she's back with him. I hate her. I hate him. If I didn't love him so much, I could really, really hate him.*

"Hey, gorgeous!" Butch's voice carried from the picnic pavilion as she started back down the beach. "Come over and have some root beer."

Laura walked stiffly. The sand sifted through her sandals and scratched the soles of her feet. The night air had grown uncomfortably cool. The noise of the fireworks gave her a headache. And picturing Janelle and Morgan together in her mind knotted her stomach tightly. She relished the misery, thankful she was capable of any feelings so intense. Since Morgan had walked out the door, she worried she was incapable of ever feeling anything deeply again.

"No soda, thanks." She shook her head. *Please,* she silently implored him, *let me enjoy my misery a moment longer.* Feeling anything dispelled the numbness that had overtaken her weeks before.

"Having fun?" Kelly sat on the porch rail, swinging her feet and sharing a smile with Butch.

"Great time," Laura muttered. "Just grand."

Kelly's eyes scoured her face. "You okay?"

"I'm okay."

Butch cleared the porch railing in one sideways leap, landing in front of Laura in the soft sand. "What's up, honey? You look upset."

"I just ran into Janelle up the beach and of course she had to let me know that she and Morgan are back together."

Butch dropped his eyes to stare at the ground, but not soon enough. Laura caught the look in them.

"You knew Morgan was seeing her again, didn't you, Butch?" Her voice was barely a whisper.

"Now, Laura . . ."

"Don't, Butch. Don't make any excuses. Morgan is a free man. If he wants to be with Janelle, that's his choice." Her voice quivered, but she went on. "We're all adults and we all have to make choices. Morgan has made his."

"It's you he wants, Laura." Butch's response was adamant. "But you won't compromise and he has his pride. Janelle doesn't mean anything to him. It's you he loves."

"Loved, Butch. Past tense." Her voice cracked as she attempted to sound casual. "He's made his choice now."

"He's here. I just saw him loading the barbecue grills in the back of Mike Renshaw's pickup. Why don't you go talk to him?"

"You knew he'd be here, didn't you, Butch?"

"Yep."

"Is that why you insisted on my coming?"

"Yep."

"It's a rotten thing to do to me." Laura was near tears. "You know I can't be around him. It hurts too much."

The cowboy's hands were planted on his hips and his jaw was set in determination as he scolded Laura. "Let's get the picture here, girl. You love him, but you don't want to be around him. He loves you, and he's miserable without you. Janelle was just waiting in the wings to get her claws into him. Now what in the heck are both of you doing to each other? Why can't you just bury the hatchet and get together?"

"I think we'd better go, Butch." Kelly tugged at his sleeve. "Come on, Laura, let's get our coolers and head for home. Come on."

Kelly looked over her shoulder. Butch had pointed out his brother earlier in the evening. In the grove of trees near the pavilion, Morgan Franklin had been watching their every move. As soon as he knew Laura had seen him, his arm looped around the waist of the short blonde at his side and his head tipped toward Janelle as she looked up into his face.

The veneer of nonchalance Laura had deliberately worn cracked as her eyes stung with unshed tears.

As they loaded the truck silently, the sky exploded in a frenzy of sparks, signaling the end of the fireworks display.

"Looks like everything's pretty much over," Kelly declared.

Laura felt her heart wrenching in half as she nodded in agreement.

Butch clutched the steering wheel and frowned in concentration as he turned down the road toward Laura's place. Watching her and Morgan trying to avoid each other these past weeks had worn him out. Kelly was still adapting to the thin mountain air and stared drowsily through the windshield. Laura focused out the window, her head hammering with Janelle's phrasing: *"Morgan and I, up before dawn. Morgan and I. Morgan and I . . ."*

"Let me get the coolers out of the back for you," Butch offered when they reached the house.

"I'll get one, you get one, and Laura can unlock the door," Kelly suggested.

"Let me call Tripper or he'll be jumping on you to see what's in the coolers." Tripper was the one thing that guaranteed a smile from Laura. She whistled for the dog. "Here, Trip! Come on, boy!"

They pushed the gate open and lugged the coolers up the front walk. Shadows from the bordering hedges mottled the yard and moonlight spattered random patterns across the walk. The house sat quiet and inviting after the noisy day of fireworks and crowds of party-goers.

"Tripper!" Laura called again. Was he in the pasture? He usually stayed within the boundaries of the place. It was unheard of for him to stray.

Butch creased his lips and whistled an earsplitting trill. "Tripper!" His voice carried across the darkened yard.

"Tripper!" Kelly used her hail-a-Manhattan-taxi voice.

All three of them stood transfixed, listening for the dog to bolt around the corner of the house.

Laura was the first to run toward the backyard. In the murky splotches of darkness, she could see the lawn furniture and steps leading to the back porch. Tripper's blanket lay near the stairs, unoccupied.

"Tripper! Here, boy!"

"He's probably down by the creek getting a drink," Kelly suggested.

Butch nodded in agreement. "Or maybe he's wandered over to Jensen's pasture."

"I don't think so," Laura answered, weariness tingeing her voice. "He went over there last month and Chuck Jensen turned the hose on him because he doesn't want other dogs around the livestock. I thought Tripper had learned his lesson."

Butch attempted reassurance. "He's around here someplace."

"He always comes when somebody drives in," Laura explained, fighting the panic rumbling deep within her. "He's always here when I get home if he doesn't go with me."

Again they called, and again. Their voices echoed in the silence of the valley, punctuated only by an occasional firecracker off in the distance.

"Let's get in the house and while you ladies put things away, I'll take a walk and see if he's down in the pasture." Butch took Laura's hand. It trembled as he led her up the back porch stairs. Taking the key from her, he unlocked the door and pushed it open.

"I'll come with you."

"No, Laura. You and Kelly sit down and have a cup of coffee. I'll find Tripper for you."

No sooner were they through the door than the phone rang.

"Laura, it's Chuck Jensen. I left two messages on your machine but I wanted to catch you if I could. I figured you must've gone to the Fourth of July party."

"Just got home. How can I help you, Chuck?"

"Bob Ellis just called me." The rancher leased the land south of Jensen's, Laura recalled. She'd met him somewhere. "I thought I'd let you know so you can keep an eye on your dog, because Bob spotted a wolf on his place earlier tonight."

Her knees weakened and threatened to buckle as Laura clutched the telephone and leaned against the doorjamb.

"Did it bother his cattle?"

"Would've, if he hadn't seen it first. He fired off a couple of rounds just to scare it away. Said if it comes back again tonight, he'll have to shoot it."

"Jim, Tripper isn't home. He wasn't here when I got back from the fireworks."

"If he comes over here, I'll call you, Laura. In the meantime, I'll check down by the creek." He didn't have to tell her why. Laura remembered reading that wolves would follow the creek to catch wildlife coming to water.

"Please, Chuck. Call me right away if you see Tripper." A wave of nausea swept over her, tingling her throat and gagging her. She never should have left him home alone. The young German shepherd would be no match for a powerful wolf.

"Laura?" Kelly's voice was thick with concern.

"A wolf was spotted at the Ellis place earlier tonight. Probably one that's crossed the line from Yellowstone Park. And now Tripper's gone." Her words were staccato, pushing out one after another as the terror within her grew.

Chapter Fourteen

The watercolor purple and orange of dawn streaked the western sky when Laura fell, exhausted and brokenhearted, into bed. Their search for Tripper had turned up no trace of the dog. Hoarse from yelling for him, her lips ached from pursing to whistle for him between shouts. Walking the river's edge where it meandered through the meadow in the black of night had produced no results, save frustration.

"Let her sleep." Butch nodded toward her bedroom as Kelly filled two coffee mugs. "That pup's going to make it home on his own or not at all." His voice was grim as he considered the possibilities.

Kelly's eyes brimmed, emeraldlike and shining. "She just can't lose that dog. He means so much to her."

"We should've taken him with us." Butch blamed himself as much as he blamed anybody. He rubbed the back of his neck with one hand. "Wolves travel in packs. If one's gone over the park boundary, it'll be joined by its buddies before long. If it hasn't been already." He steeled himself as he pictured what a marauding pack could do to a calf or fawn; the young German shepherd would be no match for the strength and cunning of a solitary wolf, much less a group of snarling, aggressive beasts.

"Do you think that's what's happened . . . a wolf?" Kelly shuddered. *If this is the wild and woolly West,* she thought, *get me back to civilization.*

"That dog never gets very far from Laura's side. He'd be here now if he could be."

Frustration knotted Kelly's muscles. She rolled her shoulders in fatigue. "We've just got to keep looking when it gets light out."

The purple morning sky faded into a brightly edged lavender canopy as the sun rose over Squaw Peak, releasing vibrant rays between feathery clouds. The air was beginning to warm after the predawn coolness that had bit at their hands and faces.

"I'm going to look out along the fenceline by Jensen's pasture." Butch emptied his coffee cup in the sink and reached for his straw cowboy hat resting on the drainboard.

"May I come with you?" Kelly was at his side in an instant.

His lips settled into a somber line; his jaw clenched. "Are you prepared for what we might find?"

The woman faltered only momentarily. She recovered, a look of determination crossing her face. "Laura can't find him if the wolves have gotten him. She can't. I won't let her go through that."

"You're a good friend." Butch brought his hand up and lightly traced the springy red curl escaping from under Kelly's canvas baseball cap. He held the screen door for her, allowing her to pass.

They walked the fenceline, swishing through the dry, knee-deep grass with their eyes scanning the landscape for any trace of the dog. At the juncture of Laura's land with Jensen's, Butch stopped and looked up the road toward the mountains.

"I can't imagine that pup would run away," he said as much to himself as to Kelly.

"Where else can we look?" It seemed to Kelly, unaccustomed to wide-open spaces, that they had covered hundreds of miles in the early-morning hours.

"Let's walk up over the hill to the draw." He pulled

her hand and tucked it within his steel grip. Together they walked at the edge of the rutted road, reaching the hill as a vehicle approached from the next knob.

The rattling truck was a familiar sight to Butch as it slowed and finally rolled to a stop in front of the two pedestrians. The tall, gaunt cowboy stepped out of the pickup cab and slammed the door.

" 'Morning." His eyes went from his brother to the short redhead at Butch's side.

"Kelly." Butch turned to his companion. "This is my brother, Morgan. This here's Kelly Hancock, Laura's friend from New York."

The cowboy's hand grasped the front of his straw hat and tipped it. His drawl was low, direct. "Pleased to meet you, ma'am."

So this was Morgan Franklin, flashed through Kelly's mind. Seeing him from a distance at the picnic didn't do him justice. *Well, Laura, he* is *a big, good-looking devil. It's not hard to see how he got your attention.*

"You two are out a little early." A smile tugged at his mouth but didn't reach his eyes.

Those steel-blue eyes, Kelly noticed, looked guarded. The smile he attempted looked uncomfortable, as though it hurt to execute it.

"We're looking for Tripper. He wasn't at Laura's when we got back after the picnic last night." Butch's voice sounded small in the openness of the hillside.

Morgan scanned the meadow toward Laura's house, but not before Kelly caught the distress in his face.

"Where's Laura?" His voice was barely a croak. It was apparent it hurt the man to even speak her name.

"Asleep. I made her go to bed. She's exhausted," Kelly explained. "She covered miles in the dark last night trying to find that dog. She's worn out."

"I'm on my way to town." Morgan shifted his glance to his brother and the woman beside him. "I'll check there and see if anybody's spotted Tripper. I'll go down the river road on my way back''—he motioned toward the far side of the hill—''and if I find him I'll bring him over.''

Kelly smiled her thanks. ''When Laura wakes up, I'll let her know you're looking.''

''Morgan?'' His brother's hand paused on the man's shoulder.

''Yeah?''

''They spotted a wolf over at the Ellis place last night.''

''Does Laura know?'' All color had drained from the blue eyes, turning them to ice.

Butch nodded. ''She took the call last night.''

''Wolves,'' Morgan muttered as he rammed his hat on the thick black curls ruffling in the morning breeze. He strode toward the pickup and slammed the door savagely behind him. The engine roared as he jerked the truck into gear and sped toward the highway.

Tripper . . . Morgan . . . fields of Indian paintbrush. The dream continued. Morgan . . . Tripper . . . the gleaming yellow eyes of a wolf . . .

Laura jerked awake and focused her sleep-laden eyes on the window. It was daylight. Perspiration across her brow plastered her hair against her forehead. Her mouth tasted like pennies. *Find Tripper, find Tripper,* her heart pounded. Rising from the bed, she shook the sleep from her head and went into the kitchen.

''Kelly?''

The house was empty.

''Tripper?'' She held her breath . . . hoping, praying.

Silence overwhelmed her.

The kitchen clock's hands stretched to two-thirty. Two empty coffee cups in the sink stared back at her as she drew a glass of water.

Butch and Kelly were in the field, walking toward the house hand-in-hand. Laura's eyes squinted against the brightness of the sunshine. She couldn't detect any waving puppy tail at their side.

Stepping out onto the back porch, she shielded her eyes with her hand. The expressions on their faces registered that Tripper was still lost.

"No luck?" Her voice was heavy with emotion; she feared saying more would bring tears that would never stop.

Butch shook his head. "We'll keep on looking till we find him, honey."

Purple shadows ringed Kelly's eyes, evidence of the hours spent in pursuit of the lost dog.

"You need some rest. You've been up all night."

Kelly nodded. "Maybe I'll lie down for a couple of hours."

"I've got to run. We'll start haying next week and I want to get the crew all lined up." Butch turned to Laura. "We saw Morgan out on the road this morning. He's checking down on the river road for Tripper. He'll stop by if he hears anything."

Say anything, Laura thought. *Don't cry. Just say something.*

"Fine. That's fine." Her voice cracked with unshed tears.

She walked. And walked. Over fields, brittle and crackling in the July heat, and across dusty roads. Down into gulches where flies buzzed in the afternoon sunshine. Up and over hillsides where jack-in-the-pulpit blossoms withered in the drying breeze. To the pinnacle of Sunset Point, then down the edge of the old stagecoach trail. Late-afternoon thunderclouds developed, pushing hot air into her shoulders and turning her tongue to wool. The sky rumbled angrily as she ascended Coolidge Hill. Changing from gray to an ominous purplish-black, the clouds bullied their way across the valley and blocked the sun completely.

"Tripper! Here, boy!" Booming thunder drowned out Laura's calls. The sky continued to blacken. Lightning flashed on the horizon, then exploded again on the near side of the mountain range.

A solitary raindrop splatted against her shoulder. Then another fell. Within minutes, a torrential rain obliterated her view of the mountainside.

Scrambling down a rocky knoll, Laura's boots slid on the water-slickened slate. She clawed at the overhanging junipers to regain her balance. Rain and wind whipped her hair into her eyes. The taste of dust and rain mingled with her tears.

Hitting the parched earth furiously, the raindrops bounced back up to create a frenzied wall of water. The noise was deafening: the crack of lightning, the roll of thunder, and the beat of rain swelled into a tempestuous crescendo.

Her hands grew raw from abrasions. Branches slapped her as the wet, rocky trail grew treacherous.

Lightning continued to taunt her, flashing then retreating, flashing more closely, then becoming subdued. Another bolt hurled from a crack in the sky. The explosion following confirmed it had hit nearby.

The deluge continued. Rain slapped against the pine boughs sheltering the woman as she crouched in a thicket. Branches twisted above her and bobbed in a frenetic rain dance. Her clothing was drenched.

The unmistakable crack of green timber splitting tolled a lightning strike within yards of where Laura had made her descent. The air filled with the acrid smell of expended heat, then with the heady fragrance of balsam fir.

Danger from lightning and from rain-loosened rocks surrounded her. The palms of her hands were raw and bleeding. Her hair, soaking and heavy, lay in a limp braid.

Mud splatters caked her cheeks. She began to shiver violently. Something chattered, and she realized it was her teeth.

"Laura!"

In her mind, Morgan's voice echoed.

"Laura!"

Exhausted and confused, Laura swiped the water from her face as her eyes scanned the hillside.

The figure in a rain-drenched denim jacket climbed the hill, steadying himself by hanging on to shrubs growing tenuously from rock overhangs. The hand-rolled shape of his cowboy hat caught the rainwater and channeled it off the center front of the brim. The wet denim of his jeans molded to his legs.

"Morgan!"

Laura heard herself cry out his name scant seconds after her mind registered he was really here for her.

In long, swift strides, he closed the distance between them.

"What are you doing out in this storm?" he yelled above the din of the squall. Anger contorted his features. "Why didn't you stay home?"

The energy of the lightning seemed to transfer to Laura. "I have to find Tripper."

"You're not going to find him in this storm," Morgan countered. "If he's around, he's got enough sense to get out of the rain."

"Meaning I don't?" Laura's voice shook with rage.

"Meaning you'd better get off this mountain before you get fried by lightning." His huge hand closed around her upper arm as he dragged her to her feet. The warmth of his body was welcoming, if infuriating. She smarted with humiliation.

"I can make it down by myself." Laura pulled away from him and drew herself up to her full height.

"Get in the pickup," he shouted behind her. "I'll give you a ride home."

"No, you won't. I'll walk."

"The heck you will. Get in."

His hand rested against the small of her back. Her shirt was sopping wet; she could feel the strong, uncompromising firmness of his hand as he directed her toward the road where his pickup sat waiting in the clearing. Leading her to the passenger side of the truck, he opened the door and deposited her on the front seat. He rounded the front of the hood and climbed in the driver's side before looking at her again.

"You could've gotten into real trouble in this storm." The warning was issued in a subdued voice.

"I can take care of myself."

"I'm aware of that. But these summer storms can be tricky. And you're not familiar with the terrain around here."

She dared to look at him. Her heart wrenched. He was devastatingly handsome. She knew every inch of that face, and she adored it. The jaw now clenched in anger, she had once outlined with kisses.

The ignition fired and he slipped the truck into gear. They eased down the old logging road, staying within the wheel ruts which were now rapidly collecting water.

"Thank you for coming after me," she said at last, when the silence in the truck had become unbearable.

"No problem."

Until they reached the front gatepost at Laura's, neither spoke again.

"You met Kelly . . ."

"I called you . . ."

They both began simultaneously.

"You first," Morgan offered.

"Kelly mentioned she met you this morning when she was with Butch," Laura began again.

"Yep. I called a couple of hours ago to let you know I was going looking for Tripper, and Kelly said you'd gone out in the hills."

"I've got to find him."

"If the wolves haven't already."

Laura shuddered.

Morgan's face was like stone. "Now maybe you see why I feel the way I do about the wolves. They won't stay in one place. I warned you." His hurt had found a target and he used it to his advantage. For just that instant, he wanted Laura to feel a fraction of the hurt he'd been living with these past weeks.

Pain flashed in Laura's eyes like lightning.

"And what does that mean? That because I favored wolves being reintroduced into the park, I'm in some way responsible for what may have happened to Tripper? How can you even think such a thing, Morgan?" Her voice came in rapid sobs. "How can you be so cruel?" Blinded by tears, she stumbled from the truck and slammed the door with all her strength.

He felt like a real jerk, like he'd kicked her when she was already down. "Laura, wait. . . ."

"Just forget it," she shouted over her shoulder, weeping, as she ran through the rain to her front door.

The interminable heat of July carried into August, but the ever-present threat of hail never reached fruition. Local haying crews and custom combiners dotted the landscape. Farmers' necks grew brown from long hours in the unrelenting sun.

Kelly returned to New York.

Tripper had not come home.

And Morgan Franklin had thrown himself into ranch work with a vengeance. Butch walked on eggshells around his older brother. The air at the ranch was static with unspoken words, uncompromising silence.

Laura backed the videotape several frames and reviewed it more slowly. Finding the point at which she wanted to begin the next scene, she carefully logged the edit and transferred it to her master tape.

Editing the tape on exchange students from the former Soviet Union had kept her days filled. She watched images of fresh-faced young people leaving their homes in Uzbekistan and Latvia, bound for American schools. Their collective expression was one of trepidation. By the last shots of the tape, however, their shy smiles filled the frames. American clothing and hairstyles had imprinted each student. They looked so contemporary, Laura mused, so typical. The project focus was to promote peace and understanding between nations. It was an ambitious undertaking and much of the credit belonged to the youngsters. Some were as young as fifteen years old. *How brave they are!* she thought as their images flew past on the advancing tape. *How happy they look!*

Of course they can be happy, she rationalized. *They've never had their heart broken by watching Morgan Franklin walk out the door.*

She shoved her chair back from the editing table and knocked the wheeled base into a collection of tape boxes stacked behind her.

One against the next, dominolike, they fell.

Her spirits fell.

Then the tears fell.

Desolation swept over her like the rainwater of a mountain storm. *I can't even keep track of a dog, much less a child,* she thought forlornly. The pain of missing Tripper had not diminished in the weeks since he had disappeared.

No dog.

No children.

No one to come home to.

Laura slammed her hand against the back of the chair, sending it gliding across the carpet to hit another stack of tapes. *Darn you, Morgan,* she fretted, *it's all your fault. A year ago I never, ever thought I was missing anything. Now I'm hollow inside because my dog's gone and you're gone and I feel like nothing's ever going to be the same again.*

Agnes Stillman had called earlier to check, as she did each day, on the progress of the hunt for Tripper. She had stopped by several times with a pie or some fruit or just to say hello. Jason hadn't come with his mother; he missed Tripper too much to see the dog's empty blanket on Laura's back porch.

Two days ago, a wildlife biologist had shot an adult male wolf with a tranquilizer gun and had transported it back within the boundaries of Yellowstone Park.

When the phone rang, she let the peal continue until the answering machine clicked into action.

"Laura." Kelly's voice filled the room. "It's me. Just wanted to see if Tripper's come home. Call me or fax me. Love you, buddy!"

Making a grab for the receiver, Laura responded. "Kelly, hi! I was in the editing room."

"Is Tripper back?"

There was a pause before Laura answered. "No."

Her friend's crying on the other end of the line twisted at Kelly's heart. She felt so helpless, so far away.

"I'm sorry, Kelly. Man alive, I've cried more in the last two months than I have in my whole life. I couldn't keep Morgan. I couldn't keep Tripper. What am I good for?"

"Now you stop it, girl," Kelly warned her. "You're a good person and you were a good person before Morgan Franklin and Tripper ever came into your life."

"I've realized," sniffed Laura, "it wasn't much of a life until they came into it."

"A skinny cowboy whose boots scuff your wooden floors, and a lop-eared mutt that does nothing but shed fur.

You could knit a new dog out of the hair Tripper got on the couch. You call that a life?''

''Yes.'' Laura grinned through her tears, remembering. ''Yes, I do.''

They talked about Kelly's October showing in a SoHo gallery, and the latest fashions from Calvin Klein, and what was playing off-Broadway. Laura reported on Agnes's no-cook recipe for raspberry jam. Kelly asked if Jason had his braces off yet. All the people Kelly met during her Montana stay had gone straight to the redhead's heart. Almost too nonchalantly, she asked after Butch.

''I haven't seen him for a week or so,'' Laura answered. ''I guess they're awfully busy with farming.''

''Have you seen Morgan?''

''Not since that day of the storm when you were here.''

''Butch has called a couple times,'' Kelly revealed.

Laura wasn't surprised. She had watched the two become friends and knew it hadn't ended there.

''Maybe he'll come see you. . . .'' Laura began.

The telephone line clicked, signaling another incoming call.

''Call waiting,'' Laura explained.

''I'm through. Just wanted to check on you. More later,'' Kelly promised. ''Take care, sweetie.''

'' 'Bye, Kell. Thanks . . .''

Laura flashed the hookswitch on the phone.

''Hello?''

''Laura Carey, please?'' The male voice was unfamiliar.

''Speaking.''

''This is Lloyd Kessler. I've got a fishing guide business up Ransom Creek . . .''

A business solicitation, Laura thought angrily. When people weren't calling her to promote their credit cards or their politics, they were soliciting for charities or for their businesses.

''Mr. Kessler, I'm really not interested in—''

"Oh, I'm not calling to sell you a guide package. I've just gotten back from a four-week pack trip into the North Ridge wilderness area, and I brought back something I think belongs to you."

"To me?" Laura's mind raced. What could she have misplaced near the river that a fishing guide would've found? Her camera? No, it hung on its strap over the bedroom door handle.

"He's a black German shepherd pup with huge paws. He's wearing a tag with your name and phone number on it."

"Tripper?" She fumbled to grasp the phone more tightly. "Tripper! You've found Tripper?"

"We left my place the afternoon of the Fourth of July, and he must've gotten in the horse trailer. By the time we unloaded, we were clear into the entry point to the wilderness area. We noticed his tags, but I wasn't about to drive clear back down from the mountains just to drop off a stray, so we kept him in camp with us until we got back this morning."

"Where are you? Where is he?" The questions were rapid-fire, staccato. "I'll come and get him."

"Well, I'm in town at the gas station. I'll bring him to you. Somebody told me you're on the old Ziminski place."

She heard Tripper's tags clinking in the background.

"I am."

"I'll drop by with him. I'm on my way."

The fifteen-minute trip from town seemed like a two-hour wait as Laura paced between the house and the road. Twice, trucks whipped up dust as they sped past her house, bound for neighboring farms. Both times, she ran to the side of the road in anticipation, and twice she was disappointed as they failed to slow at her place.

At last, when Laura thought she could stand it no longer, a black truck slowed as it approached the house.

She heard him before she could see him: the distinctive yip-yip-yip of excitement he always emitted when he wanted to play. The dog's head poked through the opening where the window was partially rolled down.

Laura flew to the truck and opened the door. In a single bound, the dog was off the seat and into her arms.

"I take it this is your dog, all right!" Mr. Kessler laughed.

Tears of joy mingled with puppy licks.

"Oh, Tripper!" Laura crooned over and over. Nuzzling her face into the dog's fur, she relished the feel of him. The dog responded in kind, lavishing puppy kisses and wagging his tail furiously.

At length, she looked up from her hold on the dog.

"Mr. Kessler, I can't thank you enough. May I reimburse you for the food Tripper ate while he was with you?"

The burly guide shook his head and grinned broadly. "Seeing that mutt home and his owner happy is payment enough. You two take care of each other." He waved and got back in the truck.

The German shepherd raced around Laura's legs and came to rest in front of her feet, never taking his eyes off his owner.

"Welcome home, boy!" Laura snuggled the dog tightly to her and offered a silent prayer of thanks for his safe return. "I've missed you so!"

As Lloyd Kessler's truck topped the ridge and started over the hill, his rearview mirror reflected a tall, pretty woman and a wildly energetic dog entering the gate of the old Ziminski place.

Chapter Fifteen

In the weeks that followed, the dog shadowed Laura's every move. Afraid of being separated again, he refused to leave her side even in the house. People in the valley grew accustomed to seeing the woman and her dog walking near the river each evening after work.

August's heat gradually gave way to the golden, halcyon days of September. Fields had been cut and harvested. A killing frost signaled the end of flower gardens for the season. The special magic that was autumn in Montana turned leaves to flame and began building thickened, protective coats on animals. Sunset arrived earlier each evening, heralding crisp, clear nights.

October found Laura close to her editing board as two projects—one on land reclamation in the southwestern United States and another on a cottage industry quilting shop in Tennessee—kept her days filled. She spent eight, ten, sometimes twelve hours a day cutting and recording scenes. When Tripper was not at her side, he was running within the chain-link enclosure she and Butch had erected in her backyard. She had called her friend as soon as Tripper had come home. Without asking, she knew he had passed the information on to Morgan.

When the sunny, warm days the natives referred to as Indian summer evolved into overcast, dismal stretches, winter was not far behind. The second week in October ushered in a snowstorm that sugared the countryside with an inch of fresh powder.

"Wax those skis," Agnes teased Laura when she called that morning. The area slopes would be opening within a month.

Laura took a break from her job one blustery afternoon to walk Tripper. The gray wind howled around them as they trudged up the hill. It caught Laura's hair and whipped it into her face. Tripper's ears were flat against his head, keeping body heat in and wind out. The lush greenery of the meadow had been replaced by the ghostly fingers of bare branches grasping at the somber clouds.

Laura tapped the snow from her boots and unhooked Tripper's leash. The welcoming warmth of the house, with its underlying scent from firewood in the parlor, greeted them.

"Down, Tripper," she instructed the pup, who obediently found his blanket and curled up for a nap.

She wiggled out of her gloves and stuffed them in a jacket pocket. As she hung it on a peg near the door, the phone rang.

"Laura?"

"Paul! How nice to hear your voice. Where are you?"

"Chicago, and it's freezing cold!"

"We've got a cold front moving in here today, too. How're things going with you?"

"That's why I'm calling. . . ."

"Paul, if you have a job, heaven help me, I have to say no. I'm up to my eyeballs in work." As much as she could use the money, Laura realized there were only so many hours in a day, and she was booked solid.

"Could you take a few days off?"

"No way. Why?"

"What difference does it make why, if you won't do it?"

"Darn you, Paul! You know you've piqued my interest. What's up?"

"Could you . . . umm . . ." He drawled the words out slowly, enticingly. "Could you come to New York the first week in November to accept a Burlington award for *Cry Wolf*?"

"You're joking." He'd better not be joking.

Paul answered seriously. "I'm not joking."

"Don't you dare kid about this, Paul."

"I'm holding my hand in the air, Scout's honor, right now." He laughed.

"I mean it, Paul. Are you serious?"

"Gavin Norman called me this morning and told me his committee is air-expressing the letter to you. You should get it tomorrow."

"I can't believe it."

On the other end of the line, Paul chuckled. "Believe it, honey. Believe it."

"I have to make arrangements. Tripper'll have to stay with the Stillmans. I'll have to get a flight reservation. I'll have to call Kelly."

"You go do your business. I'll talk to you in a day or two. Just wanted to be the first to congratulate you." His voice told her he was smiling. "And Laura?"

"Yes?"

"You really deserve it. The wolf film was a great job, and your talents made it the success it was."

In an industry where prima donnas abounded, Paul's generosity in recognizing others' talents was a rare commodity. He was an artist and an expert, and his willingness to acknowledge the contributions of his colleagues showed he was truly a class act. Laura's admiration for him was boundless.

"Thank you, Paul. And thanks for calling. I'll talk to you soon."

It took five minutes—no, ten—for her hands to stop

shaking to the point she could punch Agnes's phone number with the news. They whooped into the phone together, then settled down to make plans. Tripper would stay with them; Carl would check Laura's house to make sure the pipes didn't freeze in case the temperature dropped below zero.

The next call was to Kelly, who laughed, then cried, then laughed again.

"I'm so proud of you, girl! I knew you could do it!"

"Kelly, it's so exciting. I've dreamed about this! When I started out in this business, I heard about people winning a Burlington and I imagined how wonderful it would be to receive such recognition. I'm overwhelmed!" Coming back down to earth, Laura added, "I don't know how I'm going to get away from here for a week, but I'll do it. I have to be there to accept the award. I wouldn't dream of having them mail it to me!"

"Absolutely not," Kelly agreed. "This is your fifteen minutes of fame."

"It's more than the award. It's knowing I've learned enough in my profession to do something really well."

"And the fact that you and Paul had the guts to tackle a subject that was not entirely popular in your part of the country." Kelly didn't know she'd struck a nerve, that the wolf reintroduction question had been the parting shot over which Morgan and Laura had argued.

The friends closed their conversation with Kelly promising to call Laura next week when travel arrangements were completed.

Should she call Morgan?

How could she not? He was the man she loved, would always love. Wasn't sharing her happiness part of love?

She picked up the phone.

Then she rested the receiver back on the hook. She hadn't spoken to him in over a month, since the day she searched for Tripper in the storm. She knew Butch told him when Tripper came back. Well, she reasoned, if Morgan Franklin wanted to talk to her, he would've called her by now.

Forget him.

Her life was back on track, Laura rationalized. She had reached a milestone in her career. Almost half the mortgage on her place had been paid off.

Yes, things were going well. They were going very well indeed.

She bent to the plaid blanket inside the parlor door and stroked the black-and-brown dog snoozing contentedly.

"Things are going great. Aren't you happy for me, Tripper?"

The dog's tail thumped twice on the wooden floor. He was happy for her.

The click of Laura's high heels echoed on marble floors as she crossed the hotel lobby. She bore little resemblance to the casually attired woman who had bought the Ziminski place.

It had been a long time since she had dressed formally, and her ankles screamed in protest at the impractical shoes matching her evening gown. Her makeup had been done in the hotel beauty shop that afternoon and felt heavy and confining on her skin. Fingernails enhanced by acrylic tips and burnished to a brilliant mauve matching the hue of her floor-length gown clutched her small evening bag. Heads turned as the tall, auburn-haired beauty made her way past the marble columns of the elegant room.

"Here's one of our honorees now." Gavin Norman, head of the Burlington Award Committee, put his hands out and welcomed her as she approached the tuxedo-clad men grouped in the foyer.

Introductions were made; congratulations were bandied about. It was, Laura reflected without false modesty, her night. As the doorman assisted them, the group entered waiting limousines for the awards ceremony on the other side of Manhattan.

Kelly's business meeting would be running late, she had warned. The perky redhead had insisted they stay in the downtown hotel because, in her words, ''Nobody'd want to catch a limo from my modest little apartment. Besides, this is a special occasion. We have to celebrate!'' So, like two teenagers on a senior ''sneak day,'' they had checked into adjoining rooms at the posh old landmark hotel.

Crystal chandeliers winked at Laura in the artificial dusk of the dining room as the group found their way to the tables near the speaker's podium. Elegant gold-banded china rested on heavy damask cloths. Candles highlighting tasteful exotic flower arrangements glittered on each table. Selections offered by a string quartet drifted lightly in the background.

Laura's excitement precluded any thought of appetite. She picked at her food, discreetly pushing her fork around in some semblance of enjoying the repast.

The tingling rap of silver against crystal signaled the beginning of the awards ceremony as the evening's speaker stepped up to the podium. Lights in the cavernous room were brightened.

A recognized leader in independent filmmaking presented a brief history of documentary films. He spoke of integrity, the need to present both sides of an issue fairly. Realizing the existence of other perspectives, no matter how disparate they might be from the filmmaker's position, was crucial. He cited pioneers in the documentary video industry, relating their contributions to the art.

Laura's eyes scanned the room. Where was Paul? Perhaps he and Kelly had connected and were together somewhere in the sea of tables behind her. She straightened her shoulders and focused attention on the speaker.

At that moment, he addressed their film.

''This film team chose to meet head-on the challenge of

a controversial subject, and to deal with it in an all-encompassing, informative study. The reintroduction of the wolf to the Yellowstone National Park ecosystem has been an expensive, exhaustive, and very controversial project. Not content to use file footage of the wild beasts, Paul Caro traveled to the forests of Yellowstone National Park to film his subjects during an actual release. His second cameraperson, who also acted splendidly as video editor, will be introduced in a moment. Now, I would like to present the Burlington Award for Outstanding Documentary Direction to Paul Caro.''

The applause was thunderous as the gray-ponytailed man graciously accepted the crystal-and-bronze award. He courteously acknowledged the Committee's honor, the support of the film's sponsors, and the cooperation of the Wyoming and Montana Departments of Fish, Wildlife, and Parks. His voice became softer, lighter, when he continued.

''I would like to say a special 'thank you' to Laura Carey, without whom this project could not have been done. Laura's work on second camera, as editor and as researcher, brought *Cry Wolf* to the attention of the American public. Laura's commitment to her beliefs, as well as her complete professionalism and dedication to the film industry, helped make this possible.'' He raised the award with both hands and smiled directly at Laura. ''A special thanks to a very special lady, Laura, and thank you, everyone.''

Laura's eyes glistened. The trip had been like a dream for her. Returning to Manhattan after more than a year away had only reinforced her love for her Montana home. The city was exciting and lively and noisy. It was filled with old friends, many of whom had come to the ceremony tonight. The air crackled with vitality. There was an energy in this part of New York that rivaled anything she had ever experienced. The noises, the smells, the excitement she remembered were in actuality amplified tenfold. New York was so alive!

Paul stepped away from the speaker's area. Greeted by well-wishers at the front tables, he made his way slowly through the crowd to Laura.

"Paul, how gracious of you!" She rose and hugged him warmly. Under the Armani tuxedo stretching across his back, Laura felt the quivering of his body. Why, Paul was nervous! How endearing it was for an industry great, a world-renowned filmmaker, to feel such vulnerability. "Congratulations," she whispered before brushing his cheek with her lips.

He smiled broadly and winked at Laura. "Get ready." he nodded toward the speaker. "I'll meet you on the dance floor afterward."

"Film schools can take raw young people and mold them into good photographers and directors and editors," the master of ceremonies continued. "But the difference between hundreds of new production members each year, and the recipient of the Burlington Award, is one thing: dedication. Talent and hard work must combine to set the wheels of production in movement. It is, however, the dedication to quality work which sets one artist apart from others in the industry. Without that dedication, without the commitment to do one's very best, quality is lost. It is a privilege to present the next award to a woman whose dedication is showcased in her work. She refused to relax her standards. Her work displays a degree of professionalism that is commendable. She has captured the beauty, intelligence, and passion of her subjects and has conveyed them brilliantly in her camerawork and editing. For these reasons, the committee awards this year's Burlington for Outstanding Video Editing to Laura Carey for *Cry Wolf.*"

Laura stood and felt her knees shake with nervousness. Her shoes were too tight. Her mouth was dry. Her hands were moist. She heard the applause over her shoulder as she walked to the front of the room. Turning to shake hands with the speaker, she surveyed the crowd of faces. The award trophy was thrust at her. Surprisingly, it was heavier than it looked.

"I am honored to receive this award." She spoke into the microphone. "My work in documentaries has been, and hopefully will always continue to be, a very exciting, rewarding part of my life. I loved working on the wolf reintroduction project. And what I learned from the wolves, I will carry throughout my life. First, don't let anyone pen you in where you don't belong. Go where your heart leads you. Second, when you're afraid, hold your head high. Because all of God's creatures were born with dignity. Third, and most important, when you find your alpha partner, mate for life. Thank you."

Applause thundered as Laura smiled at the audience, her eyes brimming with unshed tears.

Through the crowd, she saw the distinctive red hair of her old friend glint in the room's lighting. Kelly applauded wildly, smiling from ear to ear. She pulled at someone beside her, someone obliterated from Laura's view by the crowd between them.

Wending her way slowly to the back of the room, Laura's progress was impeded by well-wishers shaking her hand and offering congratulatory messages. As she drew nearer Kelly's table, the redhead ran toward Laura, engulfing her in a hug.

"Congratulations, girl!" she shrieked, and wiped a mascara-tinged tear from her eyelash. Laura was instantly touched. If Kelly wore makeup, this must be a red-letter day. Indeed, she had even replaced her T-shirt and jeans with an elegant black velvet shift.

"Thanks, Kell." Laura smiled. "I'm glad you made it. You look fabulous!"

"Somebody else wants to congratulate you," Kelly

whispered as she unfolded her arms from around Laura and stepped aside.

"Hello, Laura."

"Morgan . . ."

Chapter Sixteen

The black of Morgan's hair matched to perfection the smartly tailored tuxedo he wore. His white pleated dress shirt contrasted starkly with his deeply tanned hands and face. Warm azure eyes took in Laura's face, then traveled to the tips of her highly uncomfortable shoes and up again, slowly, approvingly. A smile tugged at his lips.

"Congratulations."

His hand went out, and she felt hers shaking as he reached for it.

Was the room still filled with people? Laura couldn't say. The moment was frozen for her: only Morgan, only here, only now.

"Join us?" He pulled a chair out and helped her sit down, while somewhere across the room, the speaker thanked everyone for coming and told them to enjoy the dancing in the adjoining ballroom.

"Paul and I are going for a drink," Kelly interrupted. "Meet us in the ballroom." She wasn't surprised when neither person at the table noticed her leave.

"I can't believe you're here." Laura found her voice at last.

"Kelly asked me to come. I didn't know if you'd want me here."

I want you everywhere. Anywhere, Laura's mind responded.

"I, uh . . . I'm, uh . . ." Trying to find the words was

174

difficult. She had rehearsed over and over in her mind what she would say, how she would say it, when she saw Morgan. "I didn't know if you'd have come if I had invited you."

"I'd go anywhere you asked." His eyes were serious. Then she saw a flicker of glee settle in them as he added, "Except when you got mad at me. I think I know where you wanted me to go then!"

"Morgan, I was terribly upset. I'm sorry."

"No apology necessary. I was an idiot to mention the wolves when you were worried enough about Tripper. Butch told me what happened."

"I was never more glad than when Tripper jumped from that outfitter's truck into my arms." Laura grinned. *Never happier until tonight when I saw you,* she added to herself.

The dining room was emptying; strains of dance music from the ballroom invited them in.

"We'd better join the others," Morgan suggested. The touch of his arm at her elbow sent a current through her body. Disappointment shot through her like an arrow; she wanted to be alone with him. No one else mattered tonight but him.

Kelly and Paul were on the dance floor. They caught Laura's attention and motioned to a table nearby.

"Your first time in New York?" she asked politely. She wanted to dispense with talking completely, to cover his lips with hers so no conversation would steal the precious moments she had with him.

"No, but my first trip in a couple of years," Morgan responded. "I'm a country boy; I never lost anything in New York."

"It's unique. I'd forgotten how exciting it can be."

Morgan's expression was guarded. "I belong in Montana."

Laura leveled her eyes at piercing blue ones across the

table. "But you're here." *And how thankful,* Laura thought, *I am for that.*

"I didn't want to decline Kelly's invitation," Morgan responded. *I didn't want to go another day without seeing you,* he wanted to add.

Couples filled the dance floor, as song after song celebrated the night. Congratulations showered Laura from people she had never met.

Laura's attempt at small talk was tepid at best. Morgan's conversation was stilted, awkward. Winning the award suddenly seemed so insignificant compared to having him at her side. But he had come only at Kelly's invitation— out of courtesy, not out of love, Laura feared. Her temples throbbed.

"Come on, you two, and dance." Kelly pulled at Morgan's arm and Paul grinned at Laura.

"I'd better be getting back to the hotel, actually." Morgan avoided looking at Laura. She was too sophisticated, too glamorous to be stuck all night with a hick from the West. "You folks have got some serious celebrating to do."

Crestfallen, Laura was silent. He didn't want to spend his evening with her. He'd come only out of courtesy, and now he was ready to leave.

"My head is pounding. I'm ready to leave as well."

"I'll catch a taxi, then. Good night, Laura." Morgan shook her hand gently.

"They've kept the committee limo in front. Let us drop you at your hotel," Laura offered. *Stay with me, Morgan,* she beseeched him silently. *Let's be ourselves instead of two strangers from out of town.*

Exiting the ballroom, the couple walked in uncomfortable silence to the stretch limo at the entrance. Morgan volunteered the name of his hotel to the driver.

"That's where I'm staying." Laura hid her delight. Every extra moment with him pleased her.

"Kelly suggested it," Morgan responded. "She picked me up at the airport shortly after midnight last night. We wanted to surprise you," he said quietly.

"Well, that you certainly did!"

Crosstown traffic was thick. To Laura, the congestion was a normal part of a day's commute. To Morgan, it was a jumbled, noisy mass of yellow taxicabs and limousines.

As they pulled up to the entrance of the hotel, Morgan turned to his companion.

"You don't need to see me up to my room," he joked. "I'm a big boy. Go back and enjoy your party."

"Nonsense." Laura rejected the idea. "I'm exhausted and my head is pounding. I'm ready to call it an evening."

They walked together to the elevator. He noticed the grace with which she walked. She was acutely aware of the admiring glances he received from women as the tall, handsome figure in evening wear passed by them.

"I'm on the eighth floor," Laura said by way of explanation as the elevator doors closed.

"So am I. I'm 824," Morgan mentioned.

"You can't be. That's Kelly's room. It adjoins mine. I'm in 826."

"That's where I am, 824." He reached in his pocket and withdrew the security card. "See? 824."

Kelly had made herself scarce all day, Laura realized. Now she knew why.

"This is it," Morgan announced when the elevator doors yawned open. "Eighth floor."

The thickly padded carpet hid their footsteps as they walked down the hall toward their wing. There was a hushed silence in the hotel, broken only by the swoosh of the elevator doors as they closed to continue the journey. They reached Laura's room, and Morgan waited while she retrieved her security card from her evening bag. She stuck the card in the slot, saw the green light when it was scanned, and withdrew it. She reached for the door handle, then turned.

"Thank you for coming all this way, Morgan. I appreciate your being here on my special night."

"I'm glad I was here. I know this award means the world to you." He smiled. He raised his hand as if to caress her, then dropped it. "Good night, Laura."

You mean the world to me, Morgan, only you. She felt her throat constrict. Could she speak? The night was over for them, and she was riddled with disappointment.

"Good night, Morgan. Thanks again." Inside the door of her hotel room, her guard collapsed. She felt a tear slide from the corner of her eye as she placed her award trophy on the table. It didn't belong there, of course. It belonged on the mantel at home. Home in Montana.

She stepped out of her evening gown and returned it to the satin padded hanger in the closet. Her shoes were discarded inside the door. Thankful to be released, her toes wiggled freely and comfortably. She slid on her oversized Montana State University T-shirt and flicked on the switch for in-room music. The skyline of Manhattan twinkled in the large picture window of the suite, so like and yet so different from the starry skies at home.

A knock interrupted her reverie. The connecting door to the adjoining room—to Morgan's room—came into sharp focus as she heard the rap again.

"Morgan?" She turned the deadbolt lock and opened the door.

With her heels off and standing barefooted, she had to look up at him. He filled the doorway with his size. The tuxedo tie had been untied and dangled around his neck; otherwise, he was still perfectly groomed in his evening attire.

"I forgot. I bought something for you today." His voice was quiet, seductive.

Snap out of it, Laura, she chided herself. He could sound seductive reciting the Gettysburg Address.

He held the box out in front of him and leaned against the door frame.

"Would you"—Laura licked her lips nervously—"like to come in?"

"For a moment," he acquiesced. He crossed the threshold, brushing her shoulder lightly as he passed her and sat down on the loveseat.

The package was wrapped in a smart paisley gift paper and tied with a gossamer gold ribbon.

"I figured since you had acquired one trophy today, this might be appropriate. It also represents all your dreams and ambitions." He watched her pull the ribbon from the package and unwrap the surrounding tissue within.

Staring back at her, the metal nameplate read CAREY'S PLACE. The small holes at the top and bottom would allow it to be nailed on her gatepost.

"It's by an artist in SoHo. I wrote to Kelly right after she got back from Montana and asked her to order it. I figured they'd mail it when it was ready. But when I found out I'd be coming to Manhattan, I called the metalsmith and he just held it until today so I could pick it up."

"How very thoughtful, Morgan."

"I know how you hate it when people still call it the Ziminski place. I figured that'd help remind them it's yours."

"It's wonderful. I appreciate it." She was touched by his generosity, his thoughtfulness.

"Well." He put his hands on his thighs and rose slowly. "I'd better go. I'm glad you like it." He crossed the room and turned at the connecting door. "Good night, Laura."

The sounds of city traffic, so familiar yet now so foreign to Laura, reverberated through the canyon of concrete and glass. Manhattan never really perked until midnight on the weekends, and the clock beside the bed told Laura it was just past that time now. She had been in bed an hour, and had twisted and turned at least once each minute since retiring. It didn't help, if she were being honest with herself, that Morgan was through that connecting door. It was unnerving to picture him now, like that, so close.

She slid from under the covers and turned on the TV. An old movie flickered in its monochromatic majesty in the darkened hotel room. The name plate Morgan had given her lay on the footstool where she had left it. She picked it up now and traced the letters with her fingertip.

Carey's place. It drummed inside her head. *Carey's place.*

No, it wasn't the Ziminski place anymore. It was hers, and she had worked hard to get it. Now she had it. And with it, the recognition of her neighbors.

The name plate represented what she had wanted more than anything: recognition. She had achieved a Burlington Award. She had Carey's place.

And at this moment, she realized, it mattered so little. What mattered was, she had more love for one man than he would ever have again in his lifetime.

Laura paced the floor. *What are you going to do about it?* she challenged herself. *Let him go back to Montana not knowing you still love him? Swallow your pride and beg his forgiveness? Marry him?*

Laura stopped short. Her heart pounded. Marry him?

She turned toward the connecting door. *Do it, coward,* she chided herself. *Marry him or forget him.*

Lifting her clenched fist to the door, she rapped lightly. She waited a moment.

There was no response.

She tapped again, more forcefully.

A minute dragged into a lifetime as she listened for the latch to open.

The door remained closed.

She turned the handle and pushed. It swung open and she could see the bed had not been disturbed. She ventured into the room. Morgan's tuxedo jacket lay across the back of the chair. His shoes had been kicked by the door. The television set blared the news to an otherwise empty room.

"Morgan?" She turned down the volume on the TV set.

It was with no small relief that she realized his whereabouts: sounds of the shower mingled with his low, tuneless humming. Mist, thick with the fresh smell of shampoo, was escaping under the door.

Laura quickly left the room. A moment later, she returned, accomplished what she had set out to do, and retreated to her hotel room.

Morgan stepped from the shower stall, wiped the water from his eyes, and wrapped a terry towel around his waist. He grabbed another from the towel rack and covered his head, rubbing his thick black hair vigorously. Looping the towel around his neck, he examined his face in the mirror, decided he wouldn't shave before bedtime, and pulled both towels off his body.

Hotel beds were never comfortable, he thought as he turned down the covers.

He made a grab for the second pillow. He'd always been a pillow hog, since he liked to elevate his head with two.

He slid it toward him, then looked at the spot where it had been. Something had pulled under the bedspread. He threw the quilted fabric back and looked.

He smiled. He laughed. Then he read it again.

CAREY'S PLACE, the plaque read. Lying on the bed, next to where his place was, it told him more than any words could.

He made short work of the distance from that side of the room to the connecting door. Opening it slowly, he leaned his head in the room and saw her. Her legs were curled against her chest, covered by her T-shirt, which was stretched to improbable proportions as she watched an old movie on TV.

"Hey, Ms. Carey," he beckoned her softly.

"Hey, Morgan." Her eyes danced.

He leaned against the door frame and stared. "Does this mean what I think it means?" Work-roughened hands held the name plate up for her appraisal.

"It means I belong next to you. In Montana, in your life, wherever you want me. If"—her breath drew in sharply, nervously—"you still want me."

"You know the terms."

"Marriage?"

Morgan nodded. "I asked you before. You turned me down."

She exhaled carefully and looked him boldly in the eyes. "Then I'll ask you. Morgan, will you marry me?"

The small white frame house at the foot of the Bridger Mountains bustled with activity. Butch Franklin carried a potter's wheel up the steps to the back porch and put it down, whereupon his future bride shook her red head and pointed him to another spot.

Morgan Franklin carried boxes from Kelly's van into the house and deposited them in the corner. A full-grown black German shepherd shadowed his every step.

Laura Franklin, heavy with impending motherhood, looked fondly at the house which, up until her marriage two years ago when she moved out and Butch moved in, had been her home. It looked so small now, compared to the spaciousness of the ranch house at the Flying G.

At the edge of town, a moving van with the remainder of Kelly's things stopped at Stillman's store for directions.

Jason, tall and straight-toothed, pointed the way.

"Take the highway down to mile marker 61, then turn west on the dirt road and go about two miles. You can't miss it. It's the old Carey place."